CUPiD FROM THE EAST

Dear Gauri
Eternally Grateful
Dear!
9/1/2021.

DIPTI NAiK

First published in 2020 by

Becomeshakespeare.com

One Point Six Technologies Pvt. Ltd.
119-123, 1st Floor, Building J2, B - Wing, WadalaTruck
Terminal, Wadala East, Mumbai, Maharashtra, India, 400022.
T:+91 8080226699

ISBN - 978-93-90543-03-8

In loving memory of my late Father- In- law
"Konkanratna Shri Vasantrao Arjun Naik."
A true social worker who dedicated his life to education by building a school in Nerur, interior Maharashtra.

About the Author

Born in Mumbai, India. A Postgraduate in Biochemistry and Business Management, she has spearheaded organizations as Business Head in the Medical Communications arena for well over two decades. In early 2020 she decided to step back from her role as a Vice President to focus on her family(two beautiful daughters aged 19 and 11 and a loving husband) and to pursue her creative aspirations as well.

Publishing this novel penned almost a decade ago has become her immediate mission. As an avid blogger, her blogs depict her life's learnings in an engaging storytelling format. (www. mixedbaggage.blogspot.com)

Her professional journey continues as a Consultant, making positive changes to people's lives and businesses. Other than her pride in Indian values and culture, women empowerment is another area close to her heart.

Acknowledgement

My sincere gratitude to my younger daughter Anuja who is eleven now. The forced bed rest when I was expecting her and a year-long break to tend to her helped me accomplish my dream of writing. My loving and supportive husband Prasad. My elder daughter Rutuja, who has pushed me to continue writing during the postpartum ups and downs.

My MOM- my inspiration. Special thanks to Gauri, my sister-in-law, a passionate romance novel reader for critically evaluating and checking the entire novel for me.

My business friend Scarlett from the US, who gave me some valuable insights during her visits to India.

All my family and friends who kept me motivated to get it published.

My publishing team at BecomeShakespeare.com Special Thanks to corona pandemic for confining me indoor, thus giving me ample time to focus.

And above all, I thank God for his kind support to convert my dream into reality, though eleven years later.

The credits of drawing and design concept of the Get well soon card -Dipti Naik.

Chapter One

The cold, dark environment of the apartment seemed to echo Susan's state of mind. She tossed her bag on the sofa, deep in her thoughts looking at the night sky over New York. Twinkling lights streaming below at a slow pace matching the way her life seemed to crawl.

Sad, but also relieved that her new assignment would take her far away from the memories that haunted her here.

Her job with the NGO V-Kr foundation gave her many opportunities to travel to different countries. So far, she had never opted for one. But now she had to be out of here.

As she sat to plan for the new assignment she drifted into her thoughts.

How could she get into a whirlwind romance? She was always most grounded and sensible, yet she was drawn towards the careless charms of Harry.

Harry was an extremely talented dancer and a handsome fellow. His chestnut curly hair and distinctly dimpled chin added to his boyish charm. Though Susan hardly knew much about him, others seemed to rave over his achievements. V-Kr had invited him to choreograph some dances for their Annual fundraiser programme 2002. Susan being meticulous and sincere, was given the responsibility of getting the show together.

"Hi, guys! are we ready to rock?" his husky voice and his charm seemed to have worked on all the kids.

Susan had expected a rather reserved and conceit fellow; but here arrived a person most relaxed, fun-loving, and cool. She found herself drawn to his style, which was so much unlike hers.

Having lost her parents early had compelled her to grow up rather fast and hence maturing faster than anyone her age. Her guardian, Aunt Paula genuinely cared for her and tried to work out different things for her, but Susan found it mere interference.

It is different when you have your own family thought Susan.

That is the reason she loved working with the kids who were deprived of so many small things. She felt complete as if filling in the vacuum in her own life.

Harry had changed her life. His enthusiasm was

infectious. He was unpredictable, different from the routine. He showered her with extra attention. He challenged her to dance, laugh. To steal a few moments for herself. She was transformed into a girl, alien to herself. Time just flew, those four weeks of teaching the kids to dance, and the final program seemed to be a lovely dream. She looked forward to dressing up, looking good, and could feel butterflies in her stomach at the mere sight of him.

Late night after the fundraiser program when Harry dropped her home. She felt like a teenager on the prom night. As they kissed at her doorstep, she could not stop herself but give in to the desire. They were so eager that the same sofa had invitingly embraced both. The hurried undressing and their union seemed like the most obvious thing to happen.

Susan was drained. She had met her soulmate, she thought. She did not believe in one-night stands or flings and wanted to get into physical intimacy only with someone she loved and who would share a future. She knew her ideas could seem old fashioned. But since she did not have a family of her own, she longed to have one.

Also, having seen the trauma of the children of failed marriages, her notions about marriage and relationships were sorted.

She was ecstatic, she finally had someone to call her own.

"Oh, my precious princess, I can go on and on" Harry spoke huskily in her ear. She was so excited to have discovered a whole new meaning to life.

The following months were full of adventure. They would meet late or as and when their respective schedules permitted.

On one such exciting weekend Harry announced, "I am relocating to Paris on a new assignment, Extacy.i.e. fusion of abstract dance form within the Fashion Show."

"Wow! That's great.When are you back? and what do you mean by relocating?", she asked.

"Back? I always wanted to go and join Michelle" he added nonchalantly.

"Who is Michelle? "

"Miche..lle is my girlfriend. I...I thought you knew. The whole world knows. It was all over the electronic and print media. She is a supermodel."

"What about us? You cannot just tell me you are going like this" protested Susan still reeling with shock.

Harry seemed perplexed and then spoke casually.

"Michelle, is the reason for me to go to Paris. I thought you knew this all along. You all at VKr have so much information 'bout me" trying to reason.

"No! I had no clue. But Harry how can you do this to us? We get along so well. You treat me as if I have a special meaning to you. I always thought we had a future together." Susan was hurt and tears began to roll down her eyes.

"Yeah! I appreciate your views. I even find you desirable, but it never was a part of the scheme. I never committed myself to get into any type of relationship" he shrugged.

Susan sobbed furiously.

"Oh, come on!" continued Harry "Don't make me look like a bad man. We both have had a great time together."

Susan stood dumbfounded and shattered to even move. Harry tried to console her.

"Well!" he tried to pull her closer. "You should only thank me for having shown you how it is to live and love. Come on princess, let us not ruin what we have."

Susan felt repulsed. She ran as far as she could. She could hear her own heartbeat so loud that she thought her heart would explode. Feeling cheated, and angry with herself, she retreated into her shell.

Harry tried to get in touch with her a couple of times, but she avoided him. She was not interested in casual flings and hated to cling on.

Susan had learned her lesson.

Months just dragged on and without Harry Susan found her days full of boredom. So, when there was an opportunity to go on an assignment to India, she pounced upon it. She hardly cared where it was and what it entailed. She just wanted to be out of here.

Having finished all the formalities. She would finally be in a far-off place, to an unknown destination in another two days.

Chapter Two

As the flight got ready to land on the alien land, Susan tried to look at the landscape.

Oh lord! are we crashing into some village or are we dashing in a hill thought Susan. She closed her eyes out of fear and thought of all the people she loved. Her Aunt and Harry all came to her mind. His memories still hurt.

As she came out of the plane she was engulfed by a different feeling. She had gathered some information about the place, yet it was all like a big collage. Colorful outfits with smiling faces. She wondered what made them smile. Curious faces looked at her as she stood in the serpentine queue for her baggage.

She came across a potbellied small fellow holding a placard with her name.

"Hello! I am Susan Baxter" she introduced herself to the man.

"Namaste memsaab, I am Bhola. Welcome to India. Rahul sir was supposed to be here, but his wife is hospitalized, so I will take you. OK?"

As he took her to the guest house, he chatted fifteen to a dozen.

"How do you like India?" asked Bhola.

"Well! I haven't seen much in the last ten minutes to form an opinion." Susan replied.

"Oh, don't worry you will love it," he assured.

"Where am I going to be put up?" asked Susan.

"The accommodation is at Worli. That is an exceptionally good place. Centrally located, sea-facing apartment."

"Madam, I will show you around Mumbai. The Gateway of India, Dhobi Talao, Haji Ali, all Bollywood star houses" announced Bhola proudly.

"What's Bollywood star houses?"

"Our film stars, like your Hollywood stars."

"Well! I don't know any nor do they interest me." Susan not wanting to get into too much too soon.

"Theek Hai memsaab. I will show you what you will like" said Bhola not wanting to upset her.

"What does Theek Hai mean?" asked Susan.

"Theek Hai memsaab means... It's ok madam." he grinned as he felt he had enlightened her with valuable information.

It was a long way to the guest house. Susan saw disturbing sights of beggars at the traffic signals. They came to the car and begged. Children, women, lepers. They were of all kinds and refused to be shooed away.

"Don't feel pity memsaab. Not all are real. Some only beg to make easy money."

"But how do you know who is real and who isn't?"

"True, but how many can you help? I give money to lepers and transgenders, because here no one gives them a job." Bhola went on with his information. Susan felt too exhausted and must have dozed off.

"Memsaab, we have reached" he announced.

The place looked neat. A nice building with an apartment on the seventh floor facing the sea.

'How fantastic and serene!' thought Susan, she always longed for something like this.

"Memsaab you rest today and tomorrow. On Monday I will come at eight-thirty in the morning to drive you to the office."

Bhola then pointed to a small lady towards the kitchen.

“This is Chanda. She will come to cook and clean the place for you."

'Cook and clean', thought Susan 'What luxury!'

Chanda was a beautiful young lady, probably in her early twenties. Frail with big eyes and a lovely smiling face.

She wore a saree* and had a small child holding onto her pleats hiding behind her.

“Namaste Memsaab (with both palms joined together) sorry no one at my home. so got baby along ok for you ?"

Susan took some time to decipher "yes ok."

"Thank, you what will you eat veg, non veg, Chinese, burger, pizza, Indian? Please tell me before only. So, I get material from market.”

“Can you make all that? Great I will certainly tell you. What's his name ?" she asked.

*Saree-Long 5-6 yards long garment wrapped around a lady with pleats in the front and other end dangling over the shoulder.

“OM- we call him Babu” replied Chanda.

"Hi ! come here Om."

As he tried to hide, he seemed to be lost somewhere in his mom’s six-yard saree.

“Very shy. Slowly he will show all Masti” added Chanda with pride.

“Masti?” What’s that?” asked Susan.

“Masti? Mean….s pranks” replied Chanda. Making funny gestures in the air.

Susan was finding it a little strenuous to communicate. Probably only a matter of time. She gave her preferences for food and excused herself.

The entire day went about lazing around getting over the jetlag, a stroll by the seaside. On Sunday Susan decided to visit a close-by church before she could begin with her work. It was a lovely church but packed to the brim. She would prefer someplace quieter. Susan loved what she had seen so far.

“Good morning Memsaab, you look fresh” greeted Bhola.

“Thanks, Bhola, how is the… person’s wife” struggling to remember his name.

"Fine, but still hospitalized. I shall drive you to the office, please come."

The rest of the day was filled with introductions to the staff, meetings. There was a small function to induct her into the activities. Since Susan was sent on this special assignment the role here was more corporate than working at the grass-root level. Yet she loved getting her hands dirty; so, she requested to be put on a project with a more functional role. She was then introduced to Jia who was working closely on the Nipun project.

Jia was a cheerful girl. Fond of ragging people. She was the prankster around. Slim with brown eyes and a trendy short hairstyle. She had amazing confidence and dedication towards her work.

"These orphan children, mostly grown-up boys are selected as per their willingness to train others. Firstly, they are trained on various skills themselves. Once they acquire those skills, they are enrolled in the project as trainers." spoke Jia as she was introducing Susan to the Nipun Project.

"The new assignment or project is to help these kids to replicate their skills to youth in some interior villages to make them self-reliant" concluded Jia.

"This whole activity needs corporate funding. As you have shown keenness to be closely involved, you may both work on this project and develop the strategy for the same " finished Madam Bhaduri who was heading the India operations of V-Connect an Indian arm of V-KR.

"Sure! but why only boys as trainers?" enquired Susan.

"This work entails extensive traveling to the interiors. Firstly, we did not get any girl volunteers. Secondly, looking at the extensive travel, we have decided to enroll only boys as volunteers this time" answered Jia.

Jia was an intelligent girl with a degree in social science. She not just had the zeal to grow in her career, but also an innate desire to do good for the society.

"Madam Susan, I have drafted a list of companies that has partly been met. I will chart out the way we go about with the implementation of the program. We will be carrying out a pilot project in two villages in Maharashtra. There are no airports in these villages, no decent hotels. we will have to travel in a bullock cart. How will you manage?" asked Jia, eyes shining with mischief.

"Please call me Susan, and with a brave girl like you as my teammate. I will manage anything".

They both were probably the same age. Susan had a gut feeling that they would get along well.

After an action-packed week. Susan thought of exploring farther. During the weekend she found a quieter place to pray. It was an incredibly old beautifully built church. Though it was far, she had the solitude she wanted. She had got to know of this place from her driver Bhola. He wanted to drive her; but she insisted on going alone.

The place felt like a fairy tale. Few people were looking at her with curiosity. She sat in a corner quietly and was absorbing the atmosphere when she saw someone who probably was an American or European sitting with his feet crossed, across the other end looking at her. His features were hidden as he sat in the darker corner. She could see a stubble on a chiseled jawline. He wore an expensive stylish suit, which was not a very regular costume in India. Since she sat in a well-lit portion, it was difficult to see the man.

As she sat through the mass, she could feel that she was being watched. Once the service came to an end she quietly and quickly exited.

But she could still visualize the stranger. There was something about him, so regale. He sat as if he owned the whole place. She was ashamed to find herself thinking of someone she did not even know.

Chapter Three

Next fortnight, Susan and Jia worked tirelessly on strategizing till the last detail. The whole plan was full proof and cleared without any changes. They grew close as friends. Jia was highly principled and made few but good friends.

"Good! so next week onwards we have to run behind the sponsors. Let us have some fun tonight. My brother works for an event management company. He usually has passes and access to various events. Today is a premiere show of a Hollywood movie with some funtertainment before it. Let us go. It's a romantic movie. I am sure you would not like to miss it."

"No, Jia I would rather relax before setting out on a new mission."

"Oh, come on Susan, you have to come for my sake Please, Please, Plea…se" Jia begged with a cute expression on her face.

Finally, Susan had to give in.

The place was in a distant suburb, the event was taking place inside a huge mall. There were several westerners along with the locals.

Susan and Jia were escorted by Jia's brother Jay and her cousin Raj. Jia made them all comfortable with her sense of humor and witty remarks.

So much so that with a little coaxing from Jia, Susan participated in a few games with Jay. There were celebrities and a huge crowd of youngsters. Since it was a premier show of a romantic movie, most of the games revolved around the same theme.

When a revolving spotlight stopped on Susan, she shyly took the center stage.

"Hi, Susan" said the host. The spotlights highlighting her.

"You look fab", he added rather flirtily.

"This is Renee the other contestant. Ok! now the rapid-fire questions for both of you. Whoever wins gets couple tickets for the movie of your choice at this multiplex."

"I want you to answer fast. So, let us begin."

What qualities would you seek in the person you love?

"I .... mmm."

"Sorry! Renee no thinking."

"Trustworthy and committed" answered Susan. There was a huge applaud. Jia was screaming frantically out of excitement.

"Next question, Suppose it was your boyfriend's birthday and you had committed to going with him for dinner and coincidentally you get a chance of going to dinner with the hero of this movie, on the same day. Who would you choose?"

"The hero obviously" shrieked Renee.

Drawing mixed reactions from the crowd. Some booed, some cheered.

"Will that not upset your boyfriend?" asked the host.

"Would he miss an opportunity like this?"

Again, drawing a mixed reaction from the crowd.

"OK! now the last question. We all love our partners immensely. You both have decided to be together forever and if he were to cheat on or ditch you would you forgive or?"

"I will slap and kick him." Renee replied before the host finished and almost got into a demonstration. Drawing laughter from people around.

But Susan almost froze as she was reminded of

Harry. She carried on as if a robot. Mechanically smiling and collecting her token of participation.

Jia sensed something amiss.

"Are you ok?" she asked Susan.

"Yes", Susan had resolved not to sulk anymore. Later there was a musical chair only for celebrity couples. Since Jay was amongst the organizers, he got to be a part of it. He requested Susan to join him. The audience swooned over their favorites. Jay and Susan made it to the last five couples.

"And now ladies and gentlemen some twist to the game" announced the host.

"I want all the five gentlemen facing the girls at this end of the stage. They will be blindfolded and must walk straight to find their girls. Simultaneously we are shuffling the position of the girls too. The girls will stand with their backs, blindfolded so that they do not help their partners. The new couple will then finish the last part of the game together."

The announcement immediately caused the audience to go ecstatic, and the participants became awkward. So far, each one was only concentrating on their partners. Now each participant began to look at others as well. For Susan everyone except Jay was a stranger, as she did not know any celebrity. There was one strikingly handsome guy, probably a movie star from Hollywood she thought. As his eyes rested on Susan. She became acutely conscious. There was something peculiar about him, she had probably seen him earlier. Must be in papers or magazines. They were all blindfolded, the audience cheered and tapped on the music.

"Now guys, go get your girl."

The music had reached its crescendo and Susan could feel her pulse racing. Suddenly someone's palm rested on her nape and moved down on her shoulder as if wanting to make minimal contact. As they were asked to turn and remove the blindfold, Susan was stunned to see the stranger. His deep blue eyes were arresting. They looked around to see their respective partners.

"OH! Look at this" the host came towards Susan and addressed them directly.

"Sir, there are so many beautiful girls. But finally, you settled for someone of your kind. Well! blood is thicker than water or whatever they say" he commented trying to be funny. The crowd was cheering, and Susan could see Jia giving her a wink and a thumbs-up sign.

"Now there are three couple games to be completed. The new team will need good coordination. The fastest to complete the task shall win. The stranger quickly introduced himself "Hi, I am Dan."

"Hello, I am Susan."

They completed the first two games well and Susan was amazed by the speed and clarity of Dan's thinking. The last event was to free themselves through some ropes that entangled them. The game needed a lot of quick and close moves. Dan was working with utmost care to put Susan at ease. Yet they had to almost hug, pass from under each other's arms. He wore a lovely perfume. There was something enigmatic about him.

They lost by a fraction of a second and were adjusted as the second-best couple. They got some CDs individually. The excitement was now moving towards the screening of the movie. Some cheerleaders took over the center stage.

Jia hugged Susan and wished her. When Susan turned around Dan was nowhere. All the celebrities were whisked away for security reasons.

"Was he an actor, Jia?" asked Susan.

"Wow! he was so… handsome. I have never seen him. God knows. You liked him aah…?" teased Jia .

"No! just wondering" blushed Susan.

Chapter Four

Someone was standing in Susan's balcony.

She moved the soft curtains to see.

Dan's hair was ruffled due to the sea breeze. He turned around and invited her into his arms. Susan flew to him and they shared a passionate kiss. Their synchronization and understanding without having known each other was commendable.

"You are such a darling" he spoke in her ear causing a tingling sensation.

Trin…nng rang her alarm clock bringing her back to reality. She was ashamed of herself, one chance interaction with a stranger had impacted her so much.

"Oh, lord! Help me."

The next week was packed with corporate presentations and follow up. They had one small corporation who agreed to shell out a small sum, enough to cover the stationery cost for the entire campaign. They finished making presentations to most of the corporates shortlisted.

"We have two strong leads to follow up next week. I hope it works out. I have spoken to Mr. Sharma from Sportz INC on two occasions after the presentation. His CEO is traveling. He will let us know next week."

"Mr. Suri of Edu comp has asked us to call him on Tuesday. Then we have four smaller contributors. Good Job!" Jia further added appreciating their efforts.

"I need to unwind. Will you come to do some shopping with me tomorrow?" asked Susan.

"I cannot allow two young ladies to be on their own" said Bhola, Susan's driver with worry written largely over his face.

"Bhola, it's ok! Jia and I can manage. So, Theek Hai" Susan assured him.

"Wow! now you can speak our language too. Ok memsaab, you can call me if you need me."

The walk by the bay followed by shopping along the roadside was just the healer needed.

"Susan! why don't you try some Kurtis or Indian wear like a churidar? It's like a long shirt and a narrow tight-fitting pleated pant below it."

They leisurely strolled around the open-air stalls

which had a variety of clothes, bags, accessories, scarves, shoes everything that one would need at an affordable price.

"Come here I can tell you your future" called a roadside fortune teller sitting under a tree. He had a calm look.

"Susan, shall we? let us try this palmist. He will tell us our future" gushed Jia with excitement.

"No Jia! I do not believe it."

"Come on we do not have to take it seriously."

"You want to know your love life?" he probed.

"No! tell me whether my project and career will shape up well" asked Jia.

He kept looking at her palm, then drew his brows closer. Jia and Susan looked at each other suppressing their laughter.

"Yes, but I sense some danger too. Read *Hanuman Chalisa every day. You will get what you desire."

"You also want to know about your career?" he asked Susan.

Susan smiled feeling awkward.

*Hanuman Chalisa- Prayer book.

"Oh! this is the hand of a princess ."

There had been nothing so fortunate about her luck so far. 'I know this is all crap', thought Susan.

"All your hardships are behind you. You will excel at anything you choose because he has entered your life."

Jia and Susan looked at each other and quizzed in unison.

"He? Who he?"

"The man of your dreams. Your prince charming."

Jia raised her brow" I thought you were single."

"Of course," answered Susan and looked at him "sorry koi nahi- nobody. You are wrong."

"I can't be wrong. He is your destiny. Do not lose him, he is the best. Your true love. You will rule" and going into a trance he murmured some small prayer.

Jia just left some money and walked away. When they were out of his sight both laughed at it.

"I told you it's all an eyewash" Susan insisted.

"Little time pass is harmless" laughed Jia.

The day just seemed to pass off and both seemed to have looted the entire place.

Famished and exhausted they decided to cab it up to Susan's place.

"Why don't you stay over" suggested Susan to Jia as it was getting late.

"No, thanks. I may not be able to do so as I have not informed my mom."

"Do you live with your parents still?" quizzed Susan.

"Of course! In India, all the children normally stay with their parents. Girls go to their husband's home after marriage. Sons usually stay with their parents forever. Take care of them during their old age."

"Is that the reason there is a preference for the male child as they carry on the family name ahead or rather take care of parents during their old age?" asked Susan.

"Probably yes. The scenario has become so distorted that, in metro or big cities people are still more tolerant, but in rural areas you see a lot of female feticides" replied Jia.

"That's unfair" protested Susan.

"There are other reasons too. In some communities the parents are supposed to give away loads of money, house, car, or whatever the groom demands as dowry. The parents cannot afford it, they however must oblige. If not, then the bride is harassed mentally and physically. She may, in extreme cases be burnt or driven to commit suicide. In some communities she is merely treated as a child bearer.

Hence, a girl is considered a burden, and parents do not want a girl child" finished Jia angrily.

"Horrible! How can one discriminate like this?" Susan sounded disgusted.

"With education, self-reliance, these things are changing. That is the reason why I love our work. In metros we are blessed, but not so in the rural areas. Our work will certainly bring some change in this scenario" said Jia brightly.

"Jia! you make our work sound like we are on a crusade or some great mission" said Susan.

"Of course! and hope we get sponsorship for this mission" Jia enacted as if a commando.

"Susan! I have a question. Hope you do not mind?" asked Jia in a serious tone.

"Not at all, go on" Susan wondered what it would be.

"In your country, people are so liberal-minded,

educated. They have absolute freedom of choice in terms of career, life partner. Well! in everything. There is no discrimination between males or females. Yet, no one seems happy. We hear and read about so many affairs, divorces happening regularly."

Susan smiled "what you see or read most of the time is only about the celebrities. They do that for being in the news. It is not that the entire population is the same. And in some extreme situations dissociating is a better option. There are families with good values too. Yet somewhere in being too liberal and independent; I do feel that people have drifted apart. They have become more myopic."

Instead here, I am amazed when a financially constrained person still takes the responsibility of an ailing senior neighbour.With no expectations in return, or the stories of all the people irrespective of their religion or status coming onto the streets to help people during adversity.

"So," Susan continued "instead of blindly copying the west, if we take the family values, like unconditional love, care, affection, bonding, spiritual awareness. The innocence, spirit, patience, and purity of the East and the progress, punctuality, equality, opportunities of the West and merge them. We would have a better future."

Chapter Five

"But Mr. Sharma, you had said we shall know by Wednesday. Today is Thursday and we still have not heard from you. Please arrange for a small meeting atleast. Maybe just five minutes" Jia never sounded so low.

Susan was working up a list of new clients to be called upon.

"Oh no! we have lost two weeks and now to start all over again. I had concrete information from my friend, that Sportz INC. was keen on undertaking a philanthropic activity after the mega racing event in Malaysia. Susan, shall we barge into their office. My friend can arrange to get us in."

"Are you crazy" protested Susan.

"The project has to be rolled out as per the plan. We do not have the luxury of time. During my last discussion with Mr. Sharma, the project was approved. Then I must know what is holding it. We must hear it from the horse's mouth. Pl…e..se. We have nothing to lose. If it is a no, then we will begin with the new set of clients" promised Jia.

Despite not wanting to be a part of the adventure Susan had to give in to Jia's persistent bullying.

Both stood in a quiet corner of the CEO's office floor. Jia was informed that the meeting was scheduled to be over by six pm. The secretary would leave by five-thirty. So, they can gate crash once the delegates leave. The opulence of the surrounding, the clinical look, and the ambience was intimidating.

"Jia, I don't think we are doing the right thing. We may lose whatever little chance we have."

"Everything is fair in love and war."

"I don't think that fits here."

"Don't scare me Susan. We are running short of time and I am merely trying to eliminate a few steps. I know from an insider that the project is approved."

The watch was showing six twenty-five pm and still there was no trace of any delegates leaving.

Suddenly, they could hear the door open. They were probably some Japanese delegates, two local men guiding them. Of the lot, were two very gorgeous women in classy suits. Both Jia and Susan were amazed by the style and confidence they exuded. Their work only involved street kids, government officials and common people.

"God, I feel out of place" Jia murmured.

"Let's go back" said Jia having developed cold feet at the last moment.

"Sir, I will meet you for breakfast on Monday, before we travel back with them again. Thank you" said one local man to the person inside the room."

"Thank you" replied a deep voice.

Susan looked at Jia who was completely dumb folded.

After they all dispersed Susan suggested. "Quick, Come let's talk to him."

"No…yes. what…I mean how do we begin?"

"Jia you have to do this, remember our cause."

Susan volunteered for all the efforts they had taken to reach there.

"I... I think we are not… appropriately dressed."

"No Jia! you got to be kidding, what's wrong with you ? You can't back out now ."

"Follow me ."

Susan went to the door, but she could not get herself to barge in. She tapped gently at the door.

On getting no response she opened the door and stepped in.

"Hello…Hell…UMM…"

Chapter Six

Someone had covered her mouth and her arm was twisted behind her back. The grip was strong, and she wondered who it was. Had someone harmed Mr. Danny.

"Who are you? Who has sent you here? What do you want? And a blonde! Answer me I was not expecting anyone. How did you surpass the security? ANSWER ME NOW!" demanded the deep voice.

So, this may be Mr. Danny Brown himself thought Susan.

"Ummmm"...She shook her head violently. As he uncovered her mouth she struggled to breathe.

"Is this the way you treat your visitors?" Susan asked harshly as her back was facing him and he held her hand behind her back.

"You deserve to get better treatment from my security if this is how you visit. Who are you ?" He asked giving a small push to her hand behind her back.

"Ouch! let me go it hurts. I am from V-connect Indian counterpart of V-KR NGO. I had come to discuss the sponsorship. I...I can show you my I-card" pleaded Susan.

"No! Give me your purse. What kind of forced appointment is this?" he seemed irritated.

He pushed her closer to the desk still holding her arm. His body pressing her against the table. He emptied the entire contents of the purse on the table.

"My Identity card is in the left side pocket inside the purse. At least you could have asked me."

"All women have things dumped into their purses. It is a magic bag with cosmetics, tissues, pins, paper. Crap! yet so tiny."

"How rude!! Firstly, you look into a lady's purse and then you have the audacity to comment over it."

Suddenly his grip loosened as he was seeing her card, "Susan Baxter."

She quickly took the opportunity to drag her hand away and began to nurse her arm.

He was so close; Susan was trapped between the big oak table and him. She tried to turn around to give him a piece of her mind. However, after facing him, her irritated expressions were lost.

" You! "

His expressions looked like he was amused and surprised by her presence.

He looked so arresting with his dark hair slightly disheveled, deep blue eyes. His tie hung loose and shirt open showing his tanned neck. Susan could feel his coat brushing against her body. Instinctively Danny moved her hair that had fallen across her face.

"We meet again. I must check whether you are a planted distraction for me by my competitors. First at the church, then the mall and now here."

"Church?"

"Yes, at Colaba church."

Susan tried to recollect.

"Was it you? believe me, these are mere coincidences" she stammered as she tried to justify.

Her eyes looked large and held a genuine expression of concern.

Danny knew she was innocent. He had already

checked on her after he met her at the mall the second time. Something about her drew him towards her. He wanted to kiss her now. He looked at her. Susan felt it was like an extension of her dream.

Realizing their proximity and her discomfort Danny stepped back.

She muttered "I am sorry."

"I am sorry too, does it hurt?" he asked looking at her hand.

"Though, I still do not approve of your style of approach. Did you know that I work here?" he asked reaching for her hand.

Feeling conscious she managed to slip and sat on a chair under the pretext of putting things back in her purse.

"No! Not at all, I am sorry, but we need just ten minutes of your busy schedule to explain what we have come here for."

"We?" he repeated raising his shoulders.

"Oh yes I have my colleague Jia who is also here. Give me a second I will call her. May I Pleee...ase?"

Danny just nodded his head in agreement.

As Susan led Jia in, Jia was equally stunned to see him. She looked at the magnificent room, furniture, the deep blue carpet. The exquisite sofa, curtains, cutlery made it all look so regal. She thought he looked like an Emperor.

"This is Jia, and Jia this is Mr. Danny Brown", Susan introduced them to one another.

"Jia shall we brief him about the project?"

"Susan can you do it alone my throat is hurting, Maybe I am going to fall sick" Jia too stunned to speak.

Susan began immediately not wanting to waste any time.

"I am Susan Baxter on a special assignment from V-kr US. Here to see the exceptional work done by our Indian counterpart V-connect with regards to child education and youth empowerment. Our team in Mumbai has painstakingly over the last couple of years trained and imparted skills to the slum and street kids, which has helped them to be self-reliant and independent. Now as an ambitious gesture to make more youth self-reliant across India, we intend to replicate the model elsewhere. We have chosen some of the earlier students as the triggers or trainers who will educate the youth in our rural centers, thus making them self-reliant.

Our first phase of the project is completed, now we are rolling it out to the interior regions of India. We plan to implement this in fifteen centers across India this year, flagging off with an initial pilot project in the interiors of Maharashtra. The flag off will be in another twenty days.

The entire project report and plan had been submitted to your office more than a month back.

This is another copy for your reference. The entire logistics and financial implications have been worked out to the last detail.

The reason we have approached your esteemed organization 'Sportz INC.' is because you are a number one in the sporting arena and have made a mark of your own. In India where sports have always taken a back seat you have taken the initiative to encourage new talent. We read the article too, where you have shown an inclination to contribute to society. This would be an ideal opportunity for you to associate with a cause and empower the youth."

Danny was looking keenly at the report. There was dead silence in the room and Jia and Susan looked at each other wondering what to expect.

"I had seen this report earlier and given my consent, provided some legal and financial clarifications were done."

Had you briefed them about your deadline? I suggest you talk to Mr. Sharma on Monday morning. I will tell him to schedule an appointment with me sometime next week and in the meanwhile, he will get things rolling" offered Danny.

"Oh, Thank you Mr. Danny! We have poured our hearts into this project. It means so much. We can assure you, that your company will only stand to gain from this philanthropic activity" said Jia finding her voice.

As they got up to leave, Danny moved ahead to show them out. Suddenly the door opened, and someone flung herself at Danny.

"Hi sweetheart, I missed you."

Danny seemed embarrassed "Hi Savvy. I have some visitors leaving. This is Susan and"....

" Myself Jia. "

"Hi. Sorry but, I was informed you were alone." Her expressions did not reflect that she was sorry at all.

"I shall wait inside" she replied in a melodious voice walking towards the couch.

"Yes please" said Danny.

Once they were out Jia exclaimed "Did you see her? Wow! she looked so glamorous in that itsy-bitsy floral dress. Do you know who she is?"

"No."

"She is Savitri the new actress. She was there at the mall with Dan..Danny I mean. Her movie has done well. But I read she is single. Last week she was seen getting cozy with another famous star."

"How do you know all this?" asked Susan rather disinterested.

"Papers, magazines. She looks great but I did not like her one bit. I don't know how Danny can stand her."

"Jia, I think that's their personal lookout and remember you had to call Jay."

They stood at a local phone booth.

"Hello."

"Hi."

"Great."

“Yes. It’s almost done.”

“When”

"Today ! now !"

“Wow! Sure. I will get Susan too.”

"Susan,Guess what ! We are are going to the inauguration of the latest pub in town.”

Chapter Seven

Susan was getting used to Jia's ways. She knew she had no way out.

"Susan, I am feeling so relieved. Calls for a celebration!"

"Yes, I feel like it too. For all the hard work we have put in. let us enjoy."

"I suggest you wear that maroon dress with intricate mirror work we got the other day. You look stunning in it, Plee…ase" pleaded Jia making a cute face.

"We will see all the rich and the famous" briefed Jia's brother Jay.

This was the second instance of meeting Jay and Jia's cousin Raj. Susan felt comfortable with them as they enjoyed a very platonic friendship. She was amazed by this kind of relationship, unlike back home, where it is usually the couple that hangs out.

In India, the families would hang out together. They celebrated festivals together, shared their sorrows.

Caring for each other was not considered as probing or interference. She could now relate to her aunt as to why she was trying to work out different things for her. It was only her aunt's love and concern and not her interference.

After a light drink, before meals they decided to hit the floor. Jia and Susan danced as if there was no tomorrow. Susan had learned a few Bollywood steps, thanks to Jia, and was already drawing appreciative glances.

Exhausted as they sat down to eat, Susan felt as if she was being watched. When she looked sideways, she saw Danny. Looking strikingly handsome in his party wear. He smiled and raised his brow as if to wish. Susan could feel her heart thud, her glowing skin now showing a beautiful blush. Jia's gaze immediately followed and she started to wave frantically. Danny excused himself from the group and came across.

"May I have the pleasure of dancing with you?"

"Of course, yes! Go on Susan" exclaimed Jia.

Susan looked at her with a scowl, smiled back at Danny, and got up to dance.

As Danny and Susan danced, they were forced to be close due to the crowd on the floor. She could feel his breath on her forehead. His musky cologne only added to his masculine charm. 'Too much! this chance meeting would only add to his planted distraction theory' she thought.

"You are looking lovely and you dance well. You can even get a break in the movies here."

"Thanks, I love what I am doing, and I think you should look for the movie option you even have a star for a girlfriend."

She suddenly regretted what she said.

"Are you genuine in your suggestion or you are jealous?" asked Danny smiling.

She sensed that she had invited trouble. Fortunately, Jia interrupted asking for a dance.

Susan came back to the table and could see Jia chatting to a dozen. Danny was paying undivided attention and even laughing at something she said, Susan wondered what.

"Hello, I am Sashi and I am looking out for a fresh face to be launched in our new movie. You seem to fit the bill right" he said handing his card to Susan.

"Sorry I am working elsewhere and not interested in movies" answered Susan.

He proved to be a pest. Jia's brother Jay and Raj asked him to stay away. Finally, not wanting to create a scene, Susan and her group left early.

To cheer Susan up and bring back normalcy Jia commented "Did you see how Savitri was clinging to the superhero, Afzal? He is such a hunk."

When I asked Danny, he laughed aloud and said "Chalta Hai"(It's OK)

"Wow! what understanding" added Raj, rather cynically.

"Understanding my foot. I think she is a parasite" commented Jia.

"You know Susan I think you two looked better together."

"Yes" said the others in unison.

"I am amazed by how we keep running into the same person. He even happens to be the Danny Brown you guys were trying to meet. I find it queer. Something like the synchro destiny I read about" commented Jay.

"Please. Let us talk of something else" said Susan firmly. Suddenly their car came to an abrupt halt.

"What happened ?" asked Jia.

Raj got out and inspected the bonnet "We need a mechanic."

After ten minutes Jia climbed out of the car to know how much longer it would take.

"I have called a mechanic. He will check it. Once the guy is here, I will drop you home in a cab. So, you don't have to wait here."

Twenty minutes later there was still no sight of the mechanic.

An SUV came to halt and two men stepped out. Raj directed Jia to get in and lock up. It was Sashi, the same person who had bothered Susan. He was drunk and spoke rudely to Jay and Raj. He tried to speak to Susan through the glass. Jay dialed the police.

Just then a Mercedes came to halt.

Danny got out and came over.

"Trouble eeh?"

He tried to put some sense into the drunken men. The police arrived on time. Danny managed to salvage the situation and got his driver to take care of Jay's car.

"I am going home. Shall I drop you guys?" he asked the group.

The entire group looked at each other as if sharing the same thoughts.

If these were coincidences, they were certainly too many.

Danny dropped Jia and her brothers and drove towards Susan's residence. They sat silently not knowing what to say. Susan felt relieved that he had come to their rescue. She stole a glance at his profile and felt he looked irritated about something. There were no personal discussions. Yet there were some undercurrents. When Danny shifted the car's gear his hand touched Susan's thigh. She drew herself closer to avoid further contact. His touch was enough to send strange sensations into her. Something must be wrong with her. 'He already has a girlfriend and I can't be so desperate' she reminded herself.

As she got out of his car, she was debating whether to invite him for a drink.

"Wou.. would you care for a drink?"she hesitated.

"Sure."

As they sat sipping iced tea Danny spoke "Don't worry, that fellow will not be bothering you again. Take my number. I don't want you to get into any trouble."

"Thanks' for your help" said Susan timidly.

Danny seemed to be in a foul mood. "Susan it's your choice finally. But I am incredibly good at judging people and from whatever little I know about you. I can say that you are not meant for Bollywood.You are not cut out for that."

"Thanks for your concern, but I have already rejected the offer. I know what I want to do" replied Susan softly but firmly.

Danny seemed relieved.

As they drifted to other topics, he shared some hilarious incidences that he encountered during his global travel. Susan laughed till her sides hurt. They discussed the fun during the couple's games. Those memories brought cheer and pleasure to both.

Just then her landline rang. Before Susan could attend to it. The voicemail became active. The speaker phone was on.

"Hello Susan! looks like you are not yet home. What!! had a good time? I told you that you make a good couple. Made for each other kinds ...sync... whatever that was, **strange destiny** types Ha...

ha...ha...Jia gave a hearty laugh. Call me when you are baaaack" adding melody to her words. And the phone went dead.

Susan in the meanwhile was running to pick up the phone, but Jia had hung up by then. She quickly took the phone off the hook and fiddled to put it on mute. Probably her cook must have come with her son and he had playfully changed some settings. But too late. Danny had heard it. She did not dare to go back.

"Sorry, please don't misunderstand. She is crazy. They are just ragging" Susan tried to explain. Her ears hot and red with embarrassment.

"Chill, friends will be friends" reasoned Danny. He had a strange grin on his face though.

As he got up to leave. He said "Susan, you look ravishing in this dress especially against the cars headlight. Those mirrors shine like stars making you look like one heavenly body yourself. Good choice and yes, do call Jia and tell her we had a great time. He came closer and kissed her tenderly, his hands on her bareback.

Danny held her away looked at her with a smile, his brows together as if not approving of the kiss and kissed her again.

His smile was charming. His eyes held a tender expression. She smiled and kissed him back.

What began into a friendly kiss turned into a passionate one. Susan was lost. Loving every moment as he kissed her mouth, forehead, her neck. She moved her palms greedily across his chest. As he fiddled with the strap of her halter neck ; she came back to her senses.

"Stop... please, I mean. sorry. Thanks for helping us tonight" blurted Susan out of breath.

Danny wished her a polite goodnight and left.

Chapter Eight

Jia followed up with Sportz INC. on Monday. She had to meet Mr. Sharma on the same day. Susan was held up in internal meetings ,so Jia and her finance person carried on with the Sportz INC. meeting.

"Hello Susan, good news. There are a few terms and conditions to be reworked. They are hard negotiators, but still it is a win-win situation. We have found our sponsor. So, our mission is on. We have a meeting scheduled with their internal team and their CEO Mr. Danny with the reworked final draft on Wednesday at four p.m. Subsequently we may have some more meetings with the team members to work out the details" informed Jia.

"What about the funds?" enquired Susan.

"That will be released after we submit the papers on Wednesday."

Wednesday was an especially important day for them. However, Susan was feeling rather under the weather. She had developed high fever and had to report sick to work.

"Hello Susan, Jia calling."

"Yes Jia" answered Susan.

"You sound awful. I called to ask if you can come only for the Sportz INC. appointment, but let it be. I shall manage."

"Thanks Jia and I am sorry."

Susan had to call the doctor home.

"Some rest and lots of fluids will make you better. These medicines may make you drowsy. Take them only at night" advised the doctor.

Chanda, her cook made some hot chicken soup for dinner.

"Don't worry madam. You will be ok faster and look someone just delivered these flowers for you" she added giggling.

"Flowers!" It was a beautiful bouquet with a Get well soon card.

Assuming Jia must have sent it, she opened to read it.

Susan sat stunned. She read it over and over again.

Missed you at the meeting today.
Signing up, cannot afford to have our best person down.
Willing to offer my personal services for a speedy recovery.
Get Well Soon,
Dan.

She could not avoid him. But why was he being so nice? Probably he was trying to be a friend and she was reading too much into it.

The medicines were working. She was feeling sleepy. She thought she could hear her phone ring but was too drowsy to lift it. On hearing it ring for the third time, she dragged herself to answer it. She looked at the caller's number and was surprised to see Danny's number.

"Hello" groggily with efforts to keep her eyes open. "Why did you take so long? I was beginning to get worried."

"These medicines ...Should be ok."

"Susan, are you alone? "asked Danny with concern.

"I am fine."

"I don't like it. I am coming over."

"Danny."

"No."

"Danny ...Dan ...listen. I am fine. Please do not worry. I will talk to you tomorrow morning" she slept happily feeling nice to be cared for.

Her phone rang again at seven o'clock in the morning.

She was irritated to be woken up.

"Good morning, sorry to disturb you."

"Danny?"

"Are you better? Just wanted to check if you..."

"Survived?" she interrupted "Yes I have" she joked.

"Happy to hear that. You may now continue to sleep. Take rest."

"Good day."

She was greeted by another bouquet when she woke up.

The next day the same routine continued a lovely bouquet and a call in the night. Susan found herself waiting for his call.

Dan had called her to check on her progress , when her doorbell rang. She went to attend to it with the phone cradled between her head and shoulder.

“Woooow! such a large bouquet, thanks. You are crazy!" she exclaimed still on her phone.

“You like it?” his voice fanned her ear. Startled, she turned to find him standing beside her.

“Today is Saturday, and I am in a mood to take care of the patient” his smile made his eyes twinkle as he spoke.

“Danny," Susan was suddenly aware that she was in her nightdress. “Come in. I will just freshen up.”

“Take your time I'm in no hurry.”

Susan came back dressed in casual jeans and a cotton shirt. She looked like she had recovered totally.

Danny was busy reading the newspaper. Someone else seeing it would find it a nice domestic scene.

"Hello mam" he said as he folded the newspaper

"What would you like for breakfast?"

"I have a cook who comes in early. So, breakfast is ready. Will you join me ? "

"I have had mine but, let me help you."

They sat at the table. Danny fussing over her appetite. Susan was now getting worried. She was beginning to like all the pampering but did not want to land herself in a mess.

"If you have no other plans can we spend the day together? "asked Danny.

"I was planning to get some fresh air, but don't know what to do?"Susan answered trying to avoid him. Hoping he wanted to stay indoors.

"Shall we go to the Jehangir Art Gallery and the Art Festival which is just adjacent to it? They have an amazing display of folk items from across India. Need to pick up a few things."

"OK" replied Susan.

The art gallery had an awesome collection of paintings depicting the spirit of India. Susan drifted away looking at the paintings. Danny went up to the artist, had a chat and chose one from the brochure.

"Superb, do you have this one here?" Danny enquired.

"Yes, it's unsold, please come. It is across this hallway right at the end." Just then someone called him. "I will come in a minute" requested the artist.

The picture seemed to have captured the right spirit. It was a group of people from a village in Rajasthan sitting under a banyan tree. He realised that Susan was looking at the same painting with great interest.

"Like it?" he asked.

Susan seemed mesmerized. "It's lovely, look at the details, the expressions, and the color. It seems so real."

"Guess what? I liked it too and sorry it's sold" announced Dan with gleaming eyes.

They strolled across the stalls at the art festival. There were lovely cane, wooden, silver, brass, and clay artifacts.

"Susan please choose one for me. I want to give it to Mrs. Diaz my housekeeper. They are moving into a new house next week. She selected an incredibly beautiful ethnic lampshade. They devoured some tempting mouth watering delicacies.

Susan went to get a herbal tattoo on her palm.

"No" fretted Danny "It can give you a cold and you are recovering from flu."

Danny bought her a lovely silk block printed scarf "this will keep the cold out" he said as he wrapped it around her.

Susan gifted him with a lovely carved photo frame.

"I am feeling tired now" complained Susan.

Danny dropped her home.

"Susan I am going to be traveling next entire week. I will be in touch. Take care." He drew her closer into a friendly hug.

"I will miss you miserably" his expressions said it all.

Susan was worried. She bid goodbye. He did not try to upset her in any way. He was an extremely handsome and successful person, with a girlfriend. Then why was he trying to get close to her? After the couple games she thought they had developed a bond like good pals. He was sharp, probably having sensed her feelings towards him, was he just flirting? Susan was not keen on getting into a casual relationship.

Chapter Nine

Susan ran to attend to the doorbell. Danny had come to see her on his way to the airport.

"Susan, he stood with hands on his hips, then running them through his hair. One entire week. I will miss you" extending his arms with a face so irresistible.

"I will miss you too" Susan ran into his waiting arms.

"I want you to be mine forever."

He spun her around and carried her into her bedroom. He traced the outline of her face sending tremors through her body. They kissed each other passionately. Susan could see the appreciative look in his eyes as he undressed her. His body was sculpted with great perfection. His lovemaking was just as tender as the patience he showed with her. He kissed her fingers and nibbled at her earlobes sending sensations that made her yearn for more. When she was wanting him to join her she moaned his name passionately into his ear "Dan please."

"I love you darling" he spoke as he kissed her wildly. Their union was truly satisfying. Dan caressed her tenderly "you are lovely my princess, I can go on and on."

Susan was sweating and restless. She sprang up. She had heard these same words earlier. What did the dream imply? she wondered. Was she getting into a similar situation?

The next entire week just dragged. Susan threw herself into work.

"What's wrong Susan? You seem to have missed work too much. Go slow" advised Jia.

For Susan, her work was her healer. Her dream has shaken her up. She had got so carried away by the attention showered upon her by Danny, that she had forgotten about Savitri his girlfriend. All these thoughts confused her. She was annoyed that he was showing such interest when he was already committed. Also angered with self for getting into a similar situation again. She had stopped responding to Danny's calls.

The official announcement to the press of the project was scheduled for the subsequent week. They were knee-deep into work. Despite having decided to wind up on Friday, the delay in printing a few mailers forced them to work on Saturday too. It was already evening, and they were getting the sets ready.

The other staff had chipped in to help them.

"Susan, we have almost finished. Shall I ask them to leave?" enquired Jia.

As the two got busy with giving final touches. Someone knocked at the door.

Both were surprised to see Danny in the doorway.

"Hello! What a surprise" sprang Jia.

"Why are you both toiling so much. No helpers?" he asked looking around.

"They just left, and this is our baby. Thanks to you" joked Jia with a wink.

"Jia! Stop it" snapped Susan.

"Sorry ."

Probably I overreacted thought Susan and turned her back towards both.

Danny looked at Jia and asked what was wrong with Susan through gestures.

"Don't worry she has not recovered from her flu at all. Maybe it is the weakness. She has been working so hard lately" whispered Jia.

Susan sat with her back fuming to be discussed like this. She only wanted to be out of this place.

"She does look tired. I think she needs someone to take good care of her till she is fit enough." Danny spoke softly yet audible enough to be heard.

Susan knew what he implied but did not dare to turn around.

"These sets are done Jia. Can I have those too?" Susan trying to keep her focus on the sets.

"Yes! I will help you" Danny offered.

As he handed her the papers, their hands touched. He looked straight into her eyes. Susan thought she could see so many questions or was it just her imagination. Shifting her focus back to her work. Susan seemed to get away for now, though only temporarily.

"OK Susan! I have finished this lot. I will quickly recheck if we have missed anything" saying so Jia walked into the adjoining room leaving the two together.

Susan was extremely conscious now. Her hand trembled .

As if sensing her discomfort Dan ordered her to sit down and helped her to the chair. She could almost feel a lump rise in her throat. She wondered why she was feeling so emotional.

Danny had moved to another part of the room as if inspecting their work.

"Danny."

He turned around in a flash happy that she had addressed him.

"We are nearing completion, and you have seen us on the job. We won't want to keep you from your other commitments."

Danny felt as if someone had given a blow in his chest. He was expecting a different response.

He was away on an assignment and had called several times, which she never responded to. He was worried sick. He had then without her knowledge, contacted Jia to know if she was well.

He had rushed to her flat on arriving back and finally come here only to see her, and all he got was a cold response.

He knew she enjoyed his company. They had parted on such a good note. Then what was bothering her? He had so many queries.

He ignored her comment and asked how the two were going home.

"Auto or Cab, Of course" replied Jia who had just wandered into the room.

"Let me have the privilege of dropping you both safely to you homes."

"But we both stay far, and it could be of inconvenience to you" objected Jia.

"Not at all."

"Suits you" said Jia before Susan could object.

She could not even give any excuse as Jia would shoot down the same. So, once they were done, she settled in the back seat of the car pretending she had a headache.

"Fine, but you will have to shift ahead once I get off " said Jia.

Susan wondered if Jia was innocently or intentionally doing this.

Why was she not wanting to get dropped later?

thought Susan. Danny could see her in the rear view mirror.

She just closed her eyes.

How far and how much could she pretend. She was a strong person, yet Danny set her pulse racing. He made her go weak in her knees. When Harry had hurt her, she dared to be firm and reject him. But with Danny, it was different. She was confused and hated it.

Jia went on with her chatting and Danny too seemed to be enjoying and absorbing all the information.

As Jia alighted Danny again asked if she would like to have dinner with them. She assured him that her mom would be waiting. He escorted her till the gate.

Susan in the meanwhile had occupied the front seat. She watched him as he walked towards the car. The headlights seemed to accentuate his chiseled looks. His most charming quality was that he made all the people around him feel comfortable. He had no airs, yet there was something regale about him.

'I have been single for too long and hence desperate' she shuddered at the mere thought.

Danny spun the car and took the route with such ease. He seemed to know all the roads well.

Susan kept her gaze fixed ahead.

Danny stopped the car along the long stretch of the sea.

“Do you have dinner ready or shall we pick something along the way?"

She was startled by such a direct question which left her with no option.

“I…I have dinner ready and can also manage to toss a salad, but I don’t think I can entertain any visitors, as I have this splitting headache.”

“Don’t worry, I am not calling anyone over." He drove on, Susan could see the irritation on his face. He seemed determined.

Chapter Ten

Susan excused herself to change into something comfortable.

She wore a lovely strappy hand-painted cotton top with a long wrap-around skirt that fit her beautifully.

Danny had already settled in a chair in the balcony overlooking the Arabian sea. The soft breeze had ruffled his hair and he seemed lost.

She could not help herself from smiling. He was fast asleep in the chair. She would have loved to touch his hair and stroke them back in their place, but instead she went towards the kitchen and began to warm the food and making a salad. As she was setting the table, she sensed him around. He was leaning against the door watching her.

She forgot her anger, headache, and all other thoughts crowding in her mind.

"Come let us have our dinner. I hope you like it."

He relaxed, feeling the genuineness in her voice.

As they were eating Danny asked, “Why did you not answer any of my calls?”

"I did see some unknown numbers, but since I was unaware... and usually I do not accept unknown calls,as I had some nuisance caller.”

“Did you go to the police?” asked Danny out of concern, before she could finish.

"No, haven't had those calls lately. I will change the number, if it persists.” she knew that sounded stupid, but she did not want to get into all that.

“Do you want a bodyguard?”

She almost choked.

“Take some water" he helped her and stroked her back as she drank the water.

She blushed as she was reminded of her dream.

He helped her clear the plates and both sat in the balcony enjoying the soft breeze.

“I love the sea view so tranquil, so soothing” commented Danny who seemed to be in no hurry. They sat quietly looking at the sea.

“Susan! I feel nice being with you. I...don’t know if it’s right on my part to ask” he spoke breaking the silence.

"Are you seeing someone or is there something bothering you?" he continued.

Susan was shocked by his questions. She wanted to say something,but was unable to hold back her tears .

"I am sorry" said Danny as he came closer to hold her in his arms. He sat holding her patiently trying to pacify her.

"Sorry Susan, it's ok" he tried to calm her.

But she was infuriated. She pushed his arms away, her eyes shone with tears and anger.

"How dare you Mr. Danny. I have a very peaceful and quiet existence. You just walk into it, make me feel nice and special. That too when you are already going steady with someone. And then you dare to ask me whether I am seeing someone? I know you are a very influential person and a shrewd business person too. All you care about is for your project to do well so that you can win accolades and good value for your shareholders. A great strategy. But I am a simple person, I was hurt once and do not want it to happen again."

Danny sat bewildered by all the allegations made by Susan. Now he knew what was bothering her. He was saddened that she had formed such wrong opinion about him.

However, the blows were not over yet, the last one was yet to come.

"You may think, I am drawn towards you. Well, maybe. I have not had physical intimacy for a long time. It could be...mere desire or lust. So don't jump to conclusions."

She repented for having said that. It sounded more like a challenge.

Danny felt deeply hurt and humiliated. As if she had abused his feelings for her.

"Fine! I will satisfy you" he said as he pulled her closer kissing her so hard. She pushed, but he went on with his savage ways. His hand pressed her closer. He could feel her, but he did not want her like this. Suddenly his grip loosened, and he let her go. She straightened herself her cheeks bright red and moist with tears. She quickly covered up as her skirt slit had moved to reveal the entire length of her leg.

"As far as your ideas about me and my girlfriend go… well. It was an understanding between the two of us. She probably has someone special by now. We did share some good times, but that is all. We called it quits long back. We are merely friends."

Susan sat dumbfounded as she knew his anger had not mellowed down. He was trying to be civic.

"Regarding getting you fired up to get better results for the project. I have good people who are doing their jobs very well. I do not need to stoop to such levels."

"But if you think the attraction is only because of some primitive unfulfilled desire. Then I think we should go for it and then decide whether it is just lust or something else" his breathing was erratic.

She looked at him confused and ashamed for making him so angry. He effortlessly lifted and took her to her bed and laid her. Before she could react, his shirt was off, and he was beside her. He kissed her gently but was holding her down firmly. She was holding back. She could feel his firm chest and was tempted to touch, but there was something wrong.

On not getting any response the force of his kisses intensified. He kissed her shoulders, her neck. He pulled at the strings of her top. Her shirt just slipped off. She could see him looking at her with awe. The exciting soft mounds of her breast heaving against the lacy bra as she breathed. He cupped and kissed them tenderly, she was filled with naked desire. Her mind and body seemed to contradict each other.

As their eyes met, Danny sensed her apprehension. He instantly moved away and sat with his back towards her.

"Susan, I do not want it to be like this" he said with his head between his hands running his fingers through his hair and elbows resting on his knees.

She did not know whether to run or see if he was ok.

He wanted her to be with him, enjoying every moment.

She knew how difficult it was for him too, but she needed time to be clear in her mind. Gratefully, she hugged his back. He could sense that she already had her shirt on.

"Thanks, I need to sort things in my mind" she said.

He picked his shirt and could see the confusion written largely on her face. "I should be leaving now, take care" he kissed her forehead and left.

Susan cried herself to sleep not knowing whether she had gained or lost something today.

The formal launch of the activity was through a press conference followed by a gala dinner.

Both Mrs. Sushma Bhaduri Head of V-connect and Mr. Danny Brown CEO Sportz INC. were seated on the stage.

Mrs. Sushma spoke about her organization; it's role and introduced Jia and Susan as the pillars of the project. They would roll out the activity in the interior of Maharashtra state as a pilot. Which could then be replicated all over the country.

Susan explained the model in detail and Jia it's impact.

Danny was impressed with Susan and Jia. They not only seemed comfortable doing the grassroots level detailed work,but also took just as effortlessly to the presentations and queries put forth by the press.

He spoke with élan about their corporate mission and introduced his public relations head to speak regarding the objective for them to sponsor such a project. The whole program went smoothly. Danny was surrounded by reporters during dinner. He could see Susan talking to some people.

She looked beautiful in a handloom saree and the chunky handicraft jewellery that she wore. Her braided hair with a small dot on her forehead made her look very Indian. He did not make any efforts to talk to her in solitude.

“Hi, there” sneaked Jia when he was alone. You spoke well.I am impressed."

Danny laughed at her remark. He knew by now Jia’s forthrightness. One could take her words at face value. He liked her as a person.

"Jia,you both did well and look stunning as well,"he added still smiling,his ears turning red.

“I am happy with the progress so far. I am sure we have funded a good cause, and that the project is in safe hands” he said extending his hand for a handshake.

Sensing the change in his tone and manner. Jia knew they had company and she excused herself.

As Danny looked through the PR file he lingered over Susan’s photo. She would be busy some where in Maharashtra. She seemed so strong and clear in her thoughts when it came to work. He was longing to meet her. He had an exhaustive travel schedule since past three weeks and another one coming up. He wanted to unwind. It was going to be a long weekend, due to some National holiday. So he decided to surprise Susan.

Chapter Eleven

A flight to Goa followed by a long grueling drive and extensive search he reached the desired location.

The village was very scenic. lush green, thatched huts, cows, bullocks and sheeps grazing leisurely. He had done so much traveling but was enthralled by the simplicity of the place. The locals looked at him disbelievingly like an odd man out. He asked a decent looking youth for Anganwadi at Kaleshwar Vidya Mandir and was directed towards a smallish roofed building up the narrow muddy road. The youth briefed other curious onlookers and they all nodded as if they were aware of who he was.

As his car was approaching the building, small children ran behind the vehicle causing a commotion. Jia and Susan came out to see the new visitor.

"Danny" yelled Jia as she ran to his car, her enthusiasm matched those of the children. "Wow! you look good even in a stubble and with the mud coating."

Susan was also excited to see him.

“Hello, what a pleasant surprise” she blushed as she came towards the vehicle smiling. She looked beautiful with the new tan.

“How did you know about our location? Did you drive all the way?” she was bombarding him with questions out of disbelief.

“Wait wait, we do not welcome our guests this way. Please come in, wash your hands and face" Jia interrupted as she guided him inside.

“How’s work?” he enquired as he sat sipping hot tea and some delicious snacks.

“We had a function in the school today morning, as it is 15th August, India's Independence day and also our last day here. The children presented some skits and songs. Now we have two days off and on Monday we report to our next centre" briefed Jia.

“Don’t worry take your time. I will look around and make myself comfortable."

Danny got a more than eager student as his guide. Who also arranged for a charpoy for Danny to relax. He took a small nap till they finished with their briefing and final paperwork. He slept peacefully on a jute charpoy(jute cot)placed under a huge banyan tree yielding shade and breeze.

When he opened his eyes there was a gathering of little admirers. Jia had kept them at bay so as not to disturb him.

Susan was talking to some ladies with a small kid parked on her waist. There were few more kids holding onto her skirt. As she turned around and walked towards him, the melee followed her. Jia looked around to see what was making him smile.

“Oh! Susan is an angel here; these are her diehard fans. Their moms literally drag them home every day. Look at Chinu baby in Susan’s arms. Isn’t she adorable?"

"You bet" not taking his eyes off Susan. Jia looked at him sharply narrowing her eyes and both began to roll with laughter.

"Can I also know what's so funny?"

Danny immediately changed the topic, not wanting to upset her in any way.

“Nothing really, but how do you travel here?” he asked Jia.

"Bullock cart or small state bus , then walk" replied Jia.

“Don’t you miss home?”

"Not really. But we do miss your company" teased Jia "Isn't it Susan?"

Susan just blushed and pretended to be busy with the baby.

She wondered what prompted Jia to make such comments with Danny around. Jia otherwise was a sober and a levelheaded girl. Danny brought out the worst in her.

Slowly the kids had mustered enough courage to come closer. They exhibited their newly acquired knowledge. Some women who had come to collect their kids spoke to Jia and bent down to touch Danny's feet.

"No stop" Danny was perplexed.

"Just hold your palm above their heads, as if to bless them. Do not worry. They are showing their respect, as you have sponsored this project for their children" explained Jia.

One old lady held his hands and spoke with her eyes moist. Danny couldn't understand a word but knew she was thanking him for the opportunity made available to her grandchildren.

Susan consoled the old lady and handed over the baby. Kissing and hugging each other amidst the sobs, the baby refused to let go of Susan. After what seemed like a tug of war. The lady managed to take the wailing child away.

Susan had tears in her eyes too. Jia stroked her back and held her hand as if to give her assurance.

Danny was touched by the way the two had bonded with all. As they walked back to the vehicle. Danny asked "how are small babies a part of this project?"

This is a rural set up these kids tag along with their siblings or is a part of the playgroup that is also a part of this building. In fact, this same building also holds school till tenth grade and night school too for the underprivileged" replied Jia with pride and awe.

After a brief spell of silence. Susan asked "Would you like to see the dam on our way back?"

She pointed towards some structures giving brief stories about the same.

"How do you remember all that ?" asked Danny.

"I find it all rather interesting. I have never seen such simple people, they genuinely care. Sometimes to the extent of irritation, but their beliefs and thoughts are so innocent and sincere.

I mean a small rock under the tree may have a peculiar shape. They may pray to it as their god "her eyes shining as she spoke." Each structure has a tale.You can't miss it. It is intriguing that there are thirty three million Gods. If you listen to some fables, you will know why they pray to animals, trees, structures. They have truly understood the significance and revere each being. Respecting and honouring each one's contribution is done by praying to them. Awesome, Isn't it?" Danny had never seen Susan so happy and relaxed.

Again, Jia and Danny looked at each other and smiled knowingly.

"What , am I boring you?" demanded Susan with her hands on her hips.

Danny was reminded of her rage. He had witnessed it the last time.

"No, just that we have never seen you so excited. I find it strange and above all, you have taken to this like a fish to the water" explained Danny.

"Oh! I always loved the outdoors, so liberating." As the three lay on the meadow, Danny shared his travel experiences, Jia shared her experiences. It seemed like an eternity between friends. Suddenly Jia saw a bullock cart and ran towards it for a ride.

"Come on" she called out aloud.

"Go on" said Danny lazily.

He rolled over to look at Susan. Her hair spread over the grass; eyes fixed on the clouds. He felt like kissing her now.

She turned her head to look at him. "Thanks for sponsoring this project. You cannot imagine the satisfaction one derives and the change that is being brought to so many lives."

She raised herself and gave a peck on his cheek. He fell back holding his heart jokingly. Susan got up and ran after Jia. Danny felt so complete.

Chapter Twelve

Danny was bowled over by the tasty dinner served. The spicy fish curry, fried fish and malvani chicken. Food satisfying all your senses. The people were loving and amazingly simple in their approach. They had organized a small campfire and sang folk songs for their entertainment.

After doing justice to the food and the events. Danny asked Susan to accompany him for a stroll. "Yes, but let's take Jia along. I do not want anyone to get wrong ideas." Danny wondered how it mattered.

Jia complained of exhaustion and asked them to carry on.

They strolled leisurely in the moonlight with their torch on. "Let's not go too far there can be wild animals roaming freely and also I have heard some awful ghost stories."

"Are you scared of ghosts?"asked Danny giving out a throaty laughter.

"Not really, but I don't want to challenge anyone" she mumbled feeling stupid. "People here begin and wind up their day early. Life is absolutely laid back " she added wanting to change the topic.

"They celebrate each festival with such pomp and pleasure. Music, food, and get-togethers form an integral part of all the celebrations. I guess, that is only to spice up an otherwise monotonous existence for them. There are no hang ups. They will ask any question without bothering whether they have invaded your privacy, but at the same time, they are equally open about themselves. You just cannot have an attitude here." She went on pouring her heart about the experiences she had so far.

"And sometimes we tend to complicate our lives so much."

She suddenly froze as if brought back to reality.

Sensing the same Danny veered the conversation towards more harmless topics.

As they walked back, they could hear some rustle in the bushes, and she moved closer to him. He put his arm around her waist as they walked. She drew away as they came closer to the houses.

Jia came running and laughing at the same time. "Guess what? since you both went for a stroll; I was left to do all the answering by myself. They asked if you both are siblings, when I answered in negative. They assumed that you are a couple and arranged for a lovely room with a poster bed, mosquito net."

"What nonsense!" interrupted Susan.

"I will sort out the confusion" offered Danny.

"Don't bother I tried, but as you know. I think it will only cause further confusion and unnecessary discussions. You guys go ahead. Later just call me and I will make some arrangements ."

"In case, I cannot help. As I may have some ladies to give me company, then do I have a word from you, Danny. That you will not take advantage of the situation?" asked Jia seriously.

"Promise" they both wanted to laugh at the absurdity but feared Susan's wrath.

Susan knew it would only complicate matters if they tried to explain things, so she gave in.

The room was beautifully lit with two lanterns and some floral arrangements . Their bags were placed near the bed.

'When did they find the time to do all this?'

wondered Susan. The ceiling was made of clay tiles with some glass tiles to allow sunlight during the day.

It all seemed so romantic thought Danny. There was a small curtained corner that served as a changing room. As they lay down to rest, a cat jumped from the roof with a thud. Susan panicked and jumped towards Danny. Her hand toppled the lantern extinguishing it. Danny checked the damage done. Thankfully, nothing caught fire. The cat too had snuggled in her bed and dozed off. They both looked at each other and laughed. Susan lay close to Danny as the light now was too dim. She feared if there would be any more nocturnal visitors.

Danny lay on the bed looking through the glass tiles.

What are you looking at?

"Anything but You."

"Sorry Danny, I have been too busy with work. I have not given this a thought at all." She knew she was lying.

He gave out a deep breath and turned towards her.

"Take your time. I do respect your feelings" he spoke as he helped ease a strand back in place from her forehead.

She closed her eye's pretending to sleep. The exhaustion of the day took over and she actually drifted off to sleep.

Danny lay awake. He hoped she could see how deeply he felt for her. He planted a kiss on her forehead. She snuggled up closer resting her head on his arm and continued sleeping, oblivious to it all.

Somewhere in the middle of the night, Susan moved as the cat purred. Her movement stirred him. He instinctively put an arm around her in his sleep. She did not want to disturb him.

She was later woken up by the rooster announcing the beginning of a new day. As she stretched, she saw Danny looking and smiling at her.

"Good Morning" he greeted her as he pecked her on her cheek. Suddenly the cat rattled by the movement jumped to start her day. Surprising both and in the process making their lips brush briefly. They could feel the strong undercurrents. Danny got up before things went beyond his control and walked towards a window that seemed nonexistent in the night. The tender sunlight lent the place a golden glow. Men were busy with their cattle. Women busy with cleaning the courtyard. Smoke bellowed from the kitchen, suggesting breakfast preparations. He was hungry already.

As they got ready to leave and finished with the final instructions to the trainers, a huge gathering had arrived to bid them farewell. Susan had her fans howling for her. She too had tears in her eyes. Danny held her hand briefly in the car to console her.

The entire day was spent exploring some forts and ruins. Danny would have to drop them and leave by Sunday noon to make it in time to Mumbai. He was constantly on the phone and attending to some issues on the laptop.

Susan was amazed by the ease with which he was handling his work without making them feel left out.

Jia teased Susan about the time they spent together. Which stopped as he walked towards them.

"They have decent accommodation. We will stay here tonight and drive down to your new location tomorrow. We will leave by six-thirty in the morning so that I can drop you and proceed to Mumbai. I have booked a room for Jia and a suite for us."

"What!" shot Susan.

Danny looked at Jia winked, and both began to roll out in laughter.

Susan blushed realizing that she was being ragged.

Their new destination seemed more advanced than the previous one, as it was a Semi-Metro compared to the earlier rural village.

“When will you be back to Mumbai?” enquired Danny.

“With this, we will be finishing the first stage. We should be back after another four weeks” answered Susan.

“We do go home for a weekend once in a while” Jia added.

“Yes, but it’s a long time. Do keep in touch” he looked at Susan and handed her a box.

"A cell phone! Why?" she protested.

“Please, to be in touch with both of you.”

His eyes held a sad expression of parting, but he smiled trying to camouflage his expressions.

“Thanks Danny, we will miss you too” said Jia.

Susan wondered whether Jia had some feelings for him. They were so comfortable almost like long lost friends.

Chapter Thirteen

The people around were as helpful as in the prior location. The classrooms were comparatively better equipped.

They had to walk for twenty minutes to reach the school. The buses would be crowded, so they decided to walk it every day.

It was during one such walk back home that Susan asked.

"Jia you always say that you will marry a person chosen by your parents, right?"

"Yes."

"But what if you found your Mr. Right, yourself?"

"Cool, I will ask him to talk to my parents first."

"And…ha.ve you found him yet?" Susan was rather surprised and wondered why she feared the answer.

"NO! why do you ask?"

"Sure? or it's too early for me to know" asked Susan.

"Susan" she continued in a serious tone.

"Firstly, I am clear that groom hunting will be done by my family. Secondly, if ever, I do like someone. You shall be the first to know. Promise."

Susan was touched. She knew Jia meant what she said.

Suddenly they heard some wolf whistles.

"These eve-teasers are a nuisance. Let us change our timings or route tomorrow" said Jia as they hurried.

Danny was busy with some new acquisition talks. The whole thing had gone off well. The last meeting held at the backwaters of Kerala gave them a day to unwind. It was a welcome change. But the memories of the lovely weekend and the wonderful night kept coming back to him. Since this time, he was away for a longer period, his mails and answering machine seemed to overflow. There were frantic calls from Savitri. Probably things had gone sour between her and her beau, but Danny did not want to be a part of it. He avoided calling back and kept to himself.

Someone desperately rang the doorbell. As he opened the door Savitri just fell into his arms. She looked sexy in the clinging outfit with the jacket missing, heavily drunk.

"Where were you darling?" she demanded.

"What's this?" he asked sharply.

She poured her heart out about how she had lost an important opportunity because of her boyfriend.

"You know I always wanted a break with the G.J. pictures, now since Afzal has an issue with those guys. He wants me to turn down the offer. That will be such a huge loss for me" she wailed.

"You both should sit and sort it out together. There will be some way out" reasoned Danny.

"I was so much better with you" she said as she flung herself at him.

"Sorry, but I sincerely feel you should sort things between the two of you."

"Don't you find me attractive anymore?"

She asked tilting her head, pouting her lips, and thrusting her cleavage provocatively."Why are you avoiding me? Is there a new woman in your life?" she probed.

Danny looked at her and said sternly "Look, we are adults. We were together for a while but, as agreed we had decided to part amicably. You have someone in your life, I too have moved on. Now I don't want any melodrama" he walked towards the main door and held it open for her. "Now Please."

She was stunned by his bluntness and stormed out of his house.

Danny fixed himself a drink. He did not like being rude, also he knew she was a nice person and hoped well for her.

****

"I am appalled at the infrastructure and the education standard meted out to these children. It's unfair" protested Susan.

"Some students are outstanding. They shine in this system too. Some fortunate ones get to go all the way and land in a city or abroad on scholarships. Some drop out due to financial and other difficulties, but hardly ever, they contribute back to society. The day that realization dawns, there will be a great change" Jia sounded sombre.

Suddenly they heard some boys whistling and commenting. They followed the two upto some distance. On seeing some people approaching they backtracked.

"I am reporting this, we need a bodyguard" Jia sounded frustrated.

"But you are used to some amount of this in Mumbai too, why worry?" asked Susan trying to make the situation light.

"Yes! but it is so safe there. One cannot follow you like this. The roads here are so deserted at times. I am more concerned about your safety."

Jia reported the matter and a bodyguard was assigned to be with them whenever they went out. He was so frail and underfed, that according to Jia, they both looked like his bodyguards. However, the plan worked as the eve-teasers kept their distance.

That evening Susan received a call from Danny he was in Venice. He enquired about their wellbeing, the progress on the project, and went on to describe the romantic boat ride, couples lost in love as if time stood still for them. Susan too was beginning to miss him. She caught herself lost in the memories of the lovely weekend they shared. She was blushing. Jia ogled to know who it was. Pretending it to be a call of no great significance, she handed the phone to Jia.

Jia updated him with all details. The eve-teasers who had been taken care of. She also went on to describe the bodyguard and joked about it. Danny did not seem very happy, but Jia assured him about their safety. So, Danny had some consolation.

It was now, almost over three weeks since Danny had seen Susan. The news in the papers bothered him immensely. Some Naxalites were killing innocent people in the Northeastern part of India. Some small tensions here and there. Susan was in a much safer place located in the southwest part of India. Yet he felt disturbed.

In the middle of the night, his phone rang wildly. He got up with a start and picked it up groggily.

He could not decipher the call initially as the man at the other end sounded frantic.

The caller realized and now repeated rather slowly. "I am Jia's brother, Susan and Jia are in some trouble. They are now at the police station. The association is doing something for their safety, but Jia asked me to inform you. I am worried can you help us, please? "

Danny dialed Susan.

"Danny help!"

"Jia calm down. Where is Susan?

Are you both OK?" he asked.

"Yes! We are safe at the police station now. There was some sort of a riot. I feel, very unsafe for us, especially Susan. We are in the Baburao University police station. Help us please."

Danny called every possible person who could be of help. The Police Commissioner, the Consulate office bearer and few other influential contacts. He took the helicopter, which could reach him the fastest. When he landed at the University ground the situation was already under control. Jia and Susan were given first aid. Susan had some bruises. She was crying as she nestled Jia's head in her lap. Jia had a bandage on her forehead with a medico attending to her. Danny quickly finished the formalities and promptly arranged for Susan and Jia to be airlifted back to Mumbai.

Chapter Fourteen

A room had already been arranged for them at the hospital.

Jia was attended to promptly. Danny had informed her family.

"She will be fine" the doctor assured, checking Susan." You can take her home, she needs rest."

As Jia's family arrived, they thanked Danny. Jia's mom hugged Susan lovingly and enquired about her wellbeing.

"She saved me and took the blows herself" wept Susan, before collapsing.

"Please, she needs rest. You may admit her here or take her home , she needs to rest "commanded the doctor.

"I will take her home" Danny insisted.

He made her comfortable on the bed in his guestroom and sat near the edge wondering how serious things would have been. He too dozed off due to sheer exhaustion.

"Jia…Jia" yelled Susan as she shivered in her sleep. Danny held her like a baby to pacify her.

In the morning Danny's housekeeper Mrs. Diaz was briefed about the new guest, her condition and put under her care till Danny would return.

Danny visited Jia at the hospital. She too was traumatized by the events of the night. On his way back he stopped at the store and got necessary things for Susan.

When he came back Mrs. Diaz was feeding her the soup.

"Thanks Mrs. Diaz, I will take charge" announced Danny. Though Mrs. Diaz did not ask, Danny could see her inquisitive expressions.

"I visited Jia; she is much better today. I have got some stuff you may need. Feel free to ask for anything else that you may need" he offered as he helped her with the soup.

"I need to go home" she said in a feeble voice.

"You are not going anywhere, "he said firmly "I cannot imagine what could have happened had Jia not called at all. Her presence of mind has saved you both."

"She risked her life for me" sobbed Susan.

"It's ok! it's all over now. You both are safe." He spoke as he held her close. "Please allow me to take care till you are fit enough to leave. Please."

Susan wanted some pampering herself but wondered if it was right to be a burden to him. His requesting tone and genuine concern softened her heart too. She nodded quietly.

Danny was out of town for the next four days. Mrs. Diaz ensured that Susan had her timely meals, medicines, and adequate rest. Danny was constantly in touch.

His apartment was huge and tastefully decorated. The sea view was amazing from the drawing-room as well as the master bedroom, which had a masculine décor suitable for his personality.

Susan decided to use the apartment's swimming pool facility. It was late afternoon. She still felt slightly sore, though there were only a few scars now. She was enjoying the swim and the solitude. Her spell was broken when she noticed Danny walking towards her in a handsome grey suit.

She was expecting him in the night. She blushed as he looked at her.

"Hi, you seem better, he was relieved to see her

coming back to normalcy. I have a business meeting now. I have come for a change. I will try to be back before eight-thirty tonight" he informed her as he held the towel for her.

His appreciative glance was enough to send her pulse racing.

How effectively she hid in the layers of clothing. The bikini's designer cut flaunted her curves.

Her wet hair gleamed; the streaks of water ran like small springs traveling down a valley. 'I hope she does not want to go home so soon' he thought to himself. She coyly accepted the towel that he was holding. She could see how difficult it was for him to act normal. They walked silently back to their apartment.

Later as he came to bid her goodbye, she could smell the cologne and his perfume. It was such an intoxicating aroma. He looked stately in his evening wear.

Mrs. Diaz had not probed but was not ignorant . She left after serving Susan her dinner by eight. On other days she had stayed over to give Susan company. Mrs. Diaz was never too fond of Savitri and felt that Susan could make a good partner, but she kept all her opinions to herself.

Chapter Fifteen

After having waited for long, Susan decided to go to bed. She changed into the lovely nightdress which Danny had arranged. 'How thoughtful of him' she wondered if he liked to see women in such satin and lace, anyway one had to appreciate his sense of style. She looked as if she had just walked out of a fashion magazine.

She settled in her bed and switched on the television to keep herself awake, but probably dozed off. When Danny walked in at nine forty-five. He could see the light and sound of the television in her room. Thinking she was awake he knocked the door gently. On not getting any response he walked in. He switched off the T.V. and came closer, she looked lovely in the nightdress. He switched off the bedside light.

Having changed and showered Danny got into his bed to sleep. He felt he heard a faint tap on the door.

He was surprised to see Susan at the door.

"Are you feeling unwell?" he asked out of concern.

She came closer and hugged him. Now he was perplexed "Are you scared? Did you have a nightmare or something?"

She held his hand and took him to his bed. She sat on the bed.

Danny sat beside her "Don't worry if you are afraid of sleeping alone. You may..."

"Danny", she stopped him by placing a finger on his lips. She looked at him with passion in her eyes and traced his lip with her finger. She then moved closer and kissed him tenderly. Danny found it impossible to resist and hoped she was aware and not under the influence of some medication. She unbuttoned his nightdress and kissed his torso, feeling it with her fingertips. He gently pulled the lacy straps exposing her breasts, so soft and beautiful. As he fondled them and moved his hands across her waist and her back. She was reminded of her dream. This was lovelier than the dream, she took his name huskily as if asking for more. He now rested her on the bed and began to explore her body. As he continued kissing and caressing, she softly called his name invitingly.

Their patient lovemaking was as pure as the dream. Susan wanted to show him how much she loved him. Finally, their wanting for each other had reached a beautiful moment, where coming together was the ultimate act. Susan felt as if she had melted into his arms and their bodies fused into one. Engulfed by the feeling of completeness, a satisfied smile played on their lips as Danny held her close caressing her.

Early in the morning Susan was woken up by Danny's movement. It was very dark outside. Susan was reminded that now it was a reality and she moved closer into his arms to feel the warmth of their naked bodies. She kissed him on his neck. He gave a satisfied grin and drew her closer.

A faint light appeared in the morning sky; Danny held her close not wanting the night to end. This time their lovemaking was more torrid and passionate than the shy beginning. Danny lifted her and took her to the bathtub. They had a lovely warm celebration surrounded by the glistening foam and the soft morning light. As he bathed and massaged her. She experienced sensations unknown to her so far. Danny was amused by the giggles and the sound of pleasure let out by her.

"I always wanted this to be special" he said as he carried her to the bed and dabbed her dry, dressing her in one of his T shirts. Enjoying every moment of it.

She looked at his strong shoulder blades and his toned muscular chest. He had a fine sculpted body like that of an athlete. He looked incredibly handsome in his wet ruffled hair. They lay lazy and tired after the passionate and fulfilling night, and fell asleep unconcerned about the world around them.

Danny was woken up by the doorbell followed by some commotion. As he got up to see what the ruckus was about.

He found Savitri, just outside his bedroom door glaring at both. Mrs. Diaz tried to pull her back, but she did not budge. Mrs. Diaz looked at Danny helplessly and walked away. Not wanting to be of any embarrassment to them.

"Good! No wonder you are not responding to my calls" she yelled sarcastically.

Susan was shocked beyond her wits. She drew the sheets close to her as if shielding herself.

Danny wanted to hold and console her, instead, he moved towards Savitri to get her out of the room.

"Why are you creating a scene?"

"I knew it was a woman. Isn't it the same babe I met at the office?" she hissed.

"You have no right to talk like this." He held her elbow and took her out of the room.

"Why, is she your new arrangement? Sorry, contract?" she yelled and burst into a peal of sharp laughter.

Danny was on the verge of losing his cool. Sensing danger, Savitri pacified and rolled her eyes.

"Well I had come to show you this" she pointed at her ring. "We are getting married this month end. You are invited," she spoke huskily moving closer as she handed him the wedding card.

"That's nice, but ...then ...Why to create such a scene?" asked Danny perplexed by her behavior.

"I hate it when I am ignored. Sorry sweetheart" She whispered touching his cheek lovingly "Bye."

"Shameless woman" muttered Mrs. Diaz.

Danny held his head in his hands, knowing what damage this may have caused " Shit!" He stood for a while outside his bedroom door and mustered some courage to walk in. Susan sat still at the edge of the bed looking at the sea. He came and sat facing her drawing her close into a hug. Susan smiled back, but he could sense the distance. Her palms resting against his chest as if an unseen wall between them.

She gave him a limp smile, pretending that there was nothing amiss. She excused herself to her room. She knew he had a concall scheduled for a couple of hours.

As she passed the drawing-room she felt ashamed to look up. What would Mrs. Diaz think of another contractual woman?'

Sometime later she informed Mrs. Diaz that she was going for a swim.

"Please eat something, you may not have the strength otherwise."

Susan quietly had a small piece of the sandwich and tea and left.

When Danny was free, he asked Mrs. Diaz if, Susan had returned. When she answered in negative. He dressed and went to the pool. There were a couple of kids frolicking in the pool. He asked the guard about Susan. According to the guard she sat for a while and went back in some time. Danny dashed off to her house only to be informed that she had left her place with some belongings.

He called Jia enquired about her wellbeing and casually asked if she had heard from Susan. Not wanting to worry her.

As he came home and sat down his phone rang. It was a local call.

"Hello Danny?"

"Susan, where are you? I am worried. Please tell me I will come to pick you up."

"I know, she replied calmly. I am ok. I need to be by myself for some time."

"How long Susan, can't you see? I have nothing to do with Savitri. She had come to give me her wedding card."

There was a long pause as if the phone were dead.

"Hello, hello" he yelled into the phone.

"I can hear you, Danny, I need some time. Sorry, Danny" she disconnected.

Danny covered his eyes and cried.

He had lost all that he thought he had within hours.

Mrs. Diaz came over and put her hand over his head.

"Don't worry; I know she loves you, but she is a simple girl and may be frightened by what she just witnessed. Once she knows her heart, she will never leave you. She is an angel."

Susan had contacted Jia but with a promise not to tell Danny. The project had taken momentum before the turn of events. She requested a posting back home on priority. All the formalities were completed and within a week she left the country for good.

Chapter Sixteen

"Susan, it's been over two months since you are back. You have overworked yourself. I am glad you have finally made some time to accompany me to my friend's place. You need a break. They have a lovely palatial place situated on the top of the hill. It will be a good vacation and a change for you" Susan's aunt reasoned with her.

"I do not need a change."

"For my sake darling, I do not know if I will stay as long to meet all of them again."

"But…Aunty you never told me about this friend earlier."

"Where do you listen to me. You seem to be lost in your own world" complained her aunt.

"They are a lovely family. We met when her kids were small. Now they may all be married and settled. I hear they will be coming too."

"I want a short and quiet vacation. We will go somewhere else. Please."

Her aunt looked at her with eyes moist, as if a

special request. Susan did not have the heart to let her down. In India and with Jia she learned the significance of valuing relations.

She missed Jia. She was in touch with her and got to know about the progress of the project. Sportz INC. was pleased with the success of the project and extended its support. She could not get herself to ask about Danny, but she wondered how he was. Not a single day passed without his memories. By now she was growing certain that she, more than liked him. She intended to call him on Christmas day to wish him and probably pour out her heart. She had let out this secret only to Jia. Even his thoughts set her pulse racing.

"Careful dear, concentrate on your driving" her aunt yelled.

It was a narrow winding road to the top. As they arrived at the gate Susan was impressed with the well-kept ground. The driveway lined by tall linear trees. A lovely fountain at the entrance of the mansion gave the place a very Victorian look. They were welcomed by an elegant couple brimming with enthusiasm. Her aunt rushed to meet her friend. Susan parked her car. All the luggage was taken care of. Her aunt introduced her to her friend Elisa. She hugged Susan. She had the kindest eyes. Her husband Clive was still so handsome. They made her feel so comfortable as if they all had known each other for a very long time.

It was a magnificent place. Susan was led into a lovely room overlooking mountains at a distance, a rose garden below the window and at the right side she could see a terrace of some other room which had lovely creepers laden with flowers.

She heard some tiny footsteps and sounds of the kids playing coming from the stairway. She felt nice as if something she had missed out on for a while. She was transported to the days she and Jia spent at the Anganwadi. Teaching children at the rural schools. Which led her to think of the beautiful weekend spent with Danny.

During lunch there were new faces. A beautiful woman Juliet, the couple's daughter and her two kids, who seemed to have taken an instant liking to Susan. Juliet was a doctor and had taken a longer vacation. Her husband was to join her later.

"Susan, will you play with us?" asked the kids. "Don't bother her" reprimanded their mom.

"Yes dear" she turned to the kids "I will play with you" assured Susan. Placing her hand simultaneously on Juliet's, to indicate it was fine.

"My son is expected after four days, he has decided to marry his cousin Ruby. It's news for us. They are to wed on New Year's Eve. It will be a simple church wedding attended only by close family. I am glad Paula you are here. You were there for his christening too, remember?"

Aunt Paula tried to recollect and then blurted " Oh! yes ...yes."

Susan was sure her aunt may have forgotten about it.

Small interesting conversations were going on around the table.

She did not want to be a part of any wedding; she would have to talk to her aunt.

During their afternoon siesta she brought up the matter.

"I am not staying till the wedding. You never told me about this."

"Oh, it is a surprise for me too. Lovely isn't it? do not panic dear. I know you may be feeling crowded. You came here only because I pestered you. Please be with me. I assure I will not make you stay a day longer than needed."

"I don't even have a decent dress" Susan knew how lame it sounded.

"Don't worry I will buy you one,may be better than the bride's" her aunt said with an excited grin and winked.Susan just rolled her eyes in hopelessness.

The children were a blessing, Susan enjoyed playing and telling stories through the evening.

After her luxurious bath post-dinner, she strolled in the garden. The place had a huge open space which was beautifully maintained. The air was chilled. One could see snow-capped mountains at a distance. She pulled her jacket's hood over her head and lay on the bench looking at the night sky.

A single tear escaped her eye. She could not get Danny out of her system.

She had herself gone to him thinking it would help her sort out her feelings for him. And when everything seemed right. The episode with Savitri just shook her up. She felt so cheap.

She believed in the sanctity of marriage and wanted it to be cherished lifelong. When she saw couples like Clive and Elisa, she felt happy. At the same time, she wondered what it would be like, had her parents been alive.

Her cellphone suddenly sprang to life "Hello." "Hello, Jia! How are you?"

"I am fine, but life's not the same without you. Have you gone on the vacation you were supposed to, with your aunt?"

"Yes! It is lovely. The people here are so good. How is everyone... I mean... at home...and office?" enquired Susan trying to be very casual.

Jia briefed her on all the developments, but not a word about Danny. Susan wondered how to bring up his topic.

"How are all at home?"

Finally, she mustered enough courage and blurted

"Jia, any news about...Danny?"

"What, you want me to tell him about the way you feel?"

"No, No. Please do not" I...I may ...I mean I will tell him myself" Susan stammered.

Chapter Seventeen

"It's a wonderful day to go riding. Isn't it?" asked Juliet.

She was an easy person to get along with. The kids were eagerly asking so many questions.

"Sometimes I feel the kids miss out on so many things being in the city" lamented Juliet.

"We are still so fortunate Juliet. I have seen kids deprived of basic necessities" answered Susan.

"You are right. We should count our blessings. Susan! would you like to go to the Children's carnival someday?" continued Juliet.

"Yes, that will be fun. Shall we go tomorrow?" asked Susan to try to fill her days with activity and doing her best to keep her promises with the kids in case she decides to leave early.

"Yes, yes!" said the children with excitement.

"I cannot come tomorrow. Let us go some other time" offered Juliet.

"NO!"... yelled the kids.

"We have a special guest coming tomorrow. Won't you like to meet him?" Juliet addressed her kids .

"Mom, we will be back soon. Please…let us go. Please... mom, please."

"No, no one can go" commanded Juliet.

"If you don't mind. I can take them to the event. We do not have many days here Juliet" offered Susan.

Juliet looked at Susan helplessly.

"How will you manage?" I will send someone to help you" she fretted.

"No need. Sam and Sally are extremely well-behaved kids. I have handled more kids at a time. I assure you,we will be fine.You will also get some solitude."

Mrs. Elisabeth was excited about her son's arrival and was making plans and giving instructions to the staff.

Susan avoided asking questions as she did not want to get too involved. However, looking at Elisabeth's excitement she had to show some interest . "Where does he stay?" she asked.

"He is globetrotting all the while. I will be seeing Jule after such a long time" she answered after a long pause and drifted to give another set of instructions.

As they were leaving for the Carnival the next morning with their picnic basket and all. Juliet asked again if she needed any help.

"Don't worry mom, I will take care of Susan and Sally!" said Sam with expressions of an adult. Diving in the seat the next moment with excitement, generating laughter all around with his innocent pranks.

"Bye, we will be fine" assured Susan again.

They spent longer at the event than expected playing on the trampoline, games, art activities. It was impossible for her to get them to leave the Carnival and could now feel the sand and paint all over herself too. She had to literally drag them back home.

As they drove back Susan could see the new cars in the car park. The kids had dozed off. The staff helped her to take the kids and the basket in. She too was feeling like soaking in the bathtub.

She expected everyone to be resting but was surprised to see everyone had gathered in the drawing-room and the place was filled with the aroma of fresh cinnamon rolls. Cake, biscuits, and tea were being served, the room was filled with noise and laughter.

"Come, Susan. I hope the kids did not bother you much" asked Elisabeth and continued to introduce."This is Ruby" she was slim, tall, and beautiful. Her off-shoulder dress highlighting her collarbones and long lean neck. Susan became acutely aware of the sand and wind that had messed with her hair and skin.

"Please pardon me. I am full of sand" and waved her hand in a casual hi.

As Susan spoke Mrs. Elisabeth addressed someone behind Susan.

"Come, dear, let me introduce you. This is Susan and Susan this is my son, Danny. We lovingly call him Jule because as a kid he also wanted to be called Juliet."

Susan had turned before Elisa had finished. She gaped in shock. Danny shook hands without bothering about the sand and showed no signs of having known her earlier. His eyes fixed and a smile plastered which seemed more like a smile on a cop's face who had nabbed some robber red-handed.

Susan was glad she had her back towards the others. Juliet invited her to join them for tea.

"You may be tired. Come here" she said making a place for her.

"No, I have to get rid of the sand or I will spoil the carpet" Susan tried to wriggle out of the situation...

"Don't worry about the carpet. That will be taken care of" Elisa offered.

Danny stood behind her like a wall.

As everyone chatted, she sneaked a glance at him. He was just as handsome except for some weight loss.

She was heartbroken that he had decided to marry. But, it was obvious. She had not spoken to him even once after the last time she spoke to him from the local phone in India.

'Then too…' she thought

"Susan!" Juliet interrupting her thoughts, "Ruby is asking you about India."

"Pardon me?"

"I am told you worked in India lately. Are there really snake charmers and animals all over? Don't you ever feel like going back? What do you cherish the most from India?" asked Ruby.

"Yes! It is a lovely country indeed. There's much more to India than just snake charmers . It is sad that we are so opinionated, we failed to realise the beauty and heritage of such a lovely country. Infact a country with lots of hope and promise."

Susan began to rub her eyes.

"I think I have some sand in my eyes please excuse me." She walked as fast as she could to her room.

How could she go through the wedding? She could not contain her emotions. Having cried her heart out, she even skipped her dinner under the pretence of a headache.

"Are you all right dear. Look at your eyes. I think it is some infection" said Aunt Paula with concern.

"I will call Juliet" she continued.

"I will be ok if I sleep, don't worry" protested Susan.

Just then there was a light tap on the door. Susan's heart skipped a beat.

"May I come in?" asked Juliet. "Sorry, dear! I think the kids may have exhausted you. I guess you should be fine with some good rest and food.

Juliet offered her a pill for her headache. Take care and rest yourself. "

Later as sleep seemed to evade her, she sat close to the window exhausted and weeping. How quickly had he forgotten her, and she was still holding onto their memories?

Feeling repulsed she cried herself to sleep. Early morning she heard a tap on her door.

She had promised the kids but had no inclination "Come in" she said reluctantly.

" Good morning Susan "wished the kids. "Oh , you are not even ready." Sam quickly climbed on the bed and sat beside her pillow. He fiddled trying to put her hair in place " Are you unwell Susan? Please come, I want you. It's really so much more fun with you". His chubby little fingers and sad face was profoundly moving.

"Don't break his heart atleast"whispered Danny angrily as he collected the kids from her bed.His proximity was enough to set her pulse racing.

She was dumbfounded. 'He is enjoying his life getting married and I am crying over something that did not even exist for him.' She thought fighting back the tears that pricked her eyes.

"We will be waiting for you downstairs, be there

in an hour" he slammed the door behind him. Leaving her with no option.

She too decided to be shamelessly casual. Doning a beautiful polo necked t-shirt and trousers that hugged her showing all her curves. She teamed it with the silk scarf gifted by Danny. Matching earrings and her hair coiled into a loose knot above her head. A few strands came out loose falling beautifully around her face. She applied some concealer around her eyes to hide the after-effects of crying.

Sam and Sally ran to her as she came to the top of the staircase. "How are you feeling now Susan?" asked Sam as he held her hand carefully. Sally clung to her leg.

Danny was reminded of the scene in the village.

The fair was enjoyed greatly especially by the kids who sat on the giant wheel dragging Susan along on all the rides.

"Mom and you sit in this dragon plea…se" requested Sally pointing with her little fingers.

Juliet developed cold feet as it was getting ready to roll out "Wait "she yelled "Danny please come. I may not be able to go on this one."

"Ruby come" coaxed Susan.

"No, No!" ... Ruby panicked.

Danny had to take the seat as other riders got restless.

The dragon moved in most abstract pattern. She could feel their thighs pressed,their weights shifting with the twists and turns. Once against him and then her. It took a three-sixty degree turn around. Susan instinctively held his arm and closed her eyes shut. Her nails dug into his arms. She was oblivious to it all.

"Susan, Susan" cheered Sam and Sally with excitement.

"You have a fan following here too" he shouted over the noise and the speed. Susan blushed and loosened her grip as she became aware.

She had to take his help to steady herself as they got off. It was certainly the most challenging ride so far.

"Thank God I did not come. I wouldn't have made it" laughed Juliet.

"Me too" said Ruby and possessively moved closer to Danny and held his hand.

"Susan you are the best "announced Sally.

"This is a lovely place for food and dance,I hear" suggested Juliet .

There was peppy folk music playing and a lot of cheering.

"Let's shake a leg" coaxed Ruby. Since it was a local folk kind of setup there were no restrictions. The locals invited Juliet and Susan. The kids too joined them. As the song came to an end, they all came to their table.

A local youth asked Susan for a dance.

"Just one dance please" he requested.

Susan was dancing with him when Sam came and pulled at his trousers "Excuse me, may I take her, her soup is getting cold."

Sam sat as close as he could to Susan.

"I am feeling jealous that both my kids have taken so much liking to you .They seem to have forgotten their mom. Isn't she an Angel?" teased Juliet poking Sam lovingly.

Danny's wry smile with an eyebrow raised felt like a dagger.

"Oh yes! with the kids" reminded Ruby placing her hand over Danny's arm.

Ruby was an attractive girl. Susan would have liked her in a normal situation, but in the given scenario she envied her more than anything.

Susan looked at Sam and Sally and asked what they would like for dessert wanting to change the topic.

It had been a very exciting day for the kids. They slept peacefully.

“Steve will be here in a few hours” announced Juliet.

“Let us go out for dinner tonight. I have not been treated for a long time" Danny teasing his sister through the rear view mirror.

"Yeah sure "offered Juliet.

Everyone was so happy, thought Susan feeling a deep sense of loss. She felt like asking him why did he not wait for her? Was he even genuine about his feelings back then? Did all the lovely times they shared together mean nothing to him?

A tear rolled out. Thanks to the sunglasses, no one could hopefully see it. She looked out and carefully dabbed her eyes not giving away. She would need to be strong. As she turned to look ahead, she saw Danny looking at her through the mirror and her heart froze. Had he seen her cry ? wondered Susan.

She avoided his gaze as they got off and got busy in helping carry the kids inside.

She was sipping her tea in her room itself when someone knocked on her door.

"Come in."

"Are you alright? asked Juliet. Ruby was accompanying her. You did not come down for tea. Steve and Jim are here. We are going for dinner."

"You guys go on. I will be with the kids" replied Susan.

"They are taken care of" said Juliet.

"Oh, come on Susan. My brother, Jim will need some company too "pleaded Ruby.

"I will feel nice if you come, it's adult time. You have been so bothered by my kids" Juliet spoke feeling guilty.

"Not at all, I am fond of them. Ok! I will come" agreed Susan as see looked at Juliet's pleading eyes.

"We are going to the club. Are you carrying an appropriate outfit or you want to try one of mine?" offered Juliet.

Juliet was so much like her brother. She had lovingly left her with no choice.

"I do have some good ones" Susan began to scan through her wardrobe.

"Hey show me that" exclaimed Ruby. "This is a very pretty dress. Is this from India?

The marron color with such intricate mirror and brocade makes it look so exotic, you must wear this" insisted Juliet.

Susan was reminded about the night at the club when Danny had complimented her for the dress and her dance. She was feeling rather nervous, as he may think she was wearing it on purpose. Then she thought to herself...' why not? Enough of sulking. Let me enjoy tonight. I may never get to see him again .' Her heart ached with the very thought. She could feel her eyes moist, but she fought back her tears.

As she climbed down, Aunt Paula announced that they were waiting for her in the car.

Susan walked towards the vehicle. The car lights came on and the car moved towards her, the headlights lent a beautiful spark to each mirror giving her a ravishing look.

"Hop in. We don't want to be late" prodded Ruby.

Susan could see the appreciative look in Danny's eyes, who was sitting beside Ruby in the front.

A good looking handsomely dressed young fellow got out of the car and held the door open for her.

"Hi! I am Jim, Ruby's brother. Thanks for agreeing to come" he smiled .

Juliet had left in the other car with Steve.

Susan could feel Danny glancing at her through the mirror. This time instead of shying away she looked back. Holding her chin up as if to challenge. He smiled and commented." Is this outfit amongst your treasure from India? It has an Indian feel to it, and you look like a heavenly body yourself."

Everyone agreed in unison.

Susan blushed and changed the topic by enquiring about Jim.

He was into Information Technology and now wanting to take up management studies along with his job. As the conversation steered ahead Jim asked Danny for guidance. Susan was impressed with Danny's depth and expanse of knowledge on the recent academic advances and clarity in thoughts.

Sometimes she felt all jumbled up in her own thoughts and wished she had such clarity especially in her personal life. She was aware of her loss. Each moment of being around him was sheer trauma. She could not stay to watch him get married to someone else. She would have to convince Aunt Paula and leave at the earliest.

Chapter Eighteen

Juliet and Steve made a lovely couple. The men were catching up on some business and political scenarios. The ambience was very lively. All tables seemed to be taken up by people who seemed to be on vacation. There was a big group of friends who looked like some sort of reunion. The music playing steered some of them to dance. Juliet looked at Steve, pleading for a dance.

"Anything for you sweetheart" Steve replied.

Jim requested Susan. He was an eager and energetic young man. He was a fine dancer. The music and cheer seemed to catch up with all. Susan loved every minute of it. She was almost transported back to her day with Jia. She felt so free. She could pour her heart to her. It suddenly struck her that she had told her about her plans to confess to Danny during Christmas. Jia was unaware of this new development and, it could complicate things for all. She panicked; all this was so unexpected that she forgot to tell Jia about the new development. She excused herself after the dance and tried to call her from the washroom.

Her efforts seemed futile as the network was too feeble.

Harried she came and walked to their table; she was too preoccupied to notice that Danny was the only occupant.

"Something bothering you?" he asked.

"No" she almost yelled out of her fear of being caught. She was avoiding his gaze looking out for others.

"You look lovely and you dance well too. You also seem very comfortable with Jim."

She wondered why he should be jealous any-more or probably try to do matchmaking for her and retorted. "Yes, he seems to be a nice and uncomplicated fellow."

"You seem to judge people too soon" his grip around his glass was a clear indication that he was irritated.

Susan looked away.

"Come dance with me. I was told we made a good couple" he challenged.

She could feel tears pricking her eyes. She had not forgotten anything nor he, yet he had moved on.

'Maybe this is the last time we dance together' she thought. As the music gained momentum, they danced closer. There seemed to be more passion and vigor to their steps. He drew her closer, she was reminded of the passionate lovemaking. She could see it in his eyes too. As he turned her hand behind her back and bent towards her,he spoke softly in her ear “You still love me and miss me. Don't you Susan?" His deep voice shaking every filament in her body.

"How dare you ask me such a question ,when you are the one marrying someone else ? "she muttered angrily. A tear escaped unknowingly. She pretended to have sprained her ankle. As others gathered, Danny asked them to continue and guided her to the table. Jim came to their rescue and asked Danny to join Ruby on the floor. Jim had come as her savior. He could lighten the atmosphere very easily.

The food was excellent, but Susan seemed to have lost her appetite.

Back in her room Susan could not get herself to sleep she sat by the window still seething with anger.

'How can he question me when he is the one moving on? I have got to set this right.' She dialed his number and asked him to meet her downstairs.

She wrapped a shawl around herself. Her ear's hot, with temper brewing inside her. They walked further away from the house. As they reached a secluded spot near a wall with creepers on it giving it a beautiful cascade effect. Danny pulled her behind the wall and looked deeply into her eyes leaning close to kiss her.

She pushed him away."How dare you?" she blurted," You are getting married to Ruby and you"...

"Stop it" Danny said firmly," I had told you what I feel for you. You said you needed time, yet not once did you bother to call. I thought you had made up your mind, and then you just vanish without any trace. What was I supposed to do? Wait? for whom? for how long?"

He pulled her closer almost pinning her against the wall.

"But now you have decided to marry, then why are you behaving like this?" she tried to wriggle out and push him at the same time.

"I am not blind Susan! at the fair, the dance, restaurant, home. I can see what you feel for me. You cried your eyes out the first day when you saw me. Can you deny it all? He held her arms forcing her to look at him."

Her tears rolled down as she was at a loss of words. "what's the point now?" she wept helplessly .

"I have always loved you. Do you even love me Susan?"

She cried resting her head against his chest.

"No Susan, I need an answer. Do you love me?" he persisted.

She moved her head in affirmation.

"Say it Susan. I need to hear it from you" he insisted shaking her in the process.

"Yes...I do love you" she confessed sobbing uncontrollably. He immediately relaxed and held her close.

After some time, Danny spoke"I know about your parents." Susan shuddered and looked at him. He could see the pain and surprise in her eyes. "Quarrels between parents can scar a child's life badly. They said they made a wrong choice and regretted it and wanted to separate. However, unfortunately, they died together in a car accident ."

"Susan, he continued. This was known only to you. No one else needs to know this. The world thinks they died as a loving, inseparable couple. It has haunted you from making any commitments. But I am sure we have tested our love and ourselves for too long. And I assure you that I love you and your idiosyncrasies too, that you display at times." There was humor in his voice. Susan felt free from a burden she had carried for so long.

"But how do you know this ?" she asked perplexed.

He smiled" your dear friend, Jia wouldn't let me into any secrets. I knew she would know something. I pestered her, but she would not budge. Surprisingly, she came to meet me and told me that you finally seemed to have made up your mind. But knowing you and your history, she was sure you could develop cold feet at the last minute. She strongly feels that we belong together and pleaded I do something. So, I arranged for this holiday by getting all into the act. I got marriage plans hoping you might panic and confess, but you are a hard nut."

"Was I the only one in dark ?" asked Susan feeling embarrassed.

"No Sam, Sally, Steve, and Jim are equally ignorant," Danny gave his devilish grin.

"I hate you for this" she pounded her fists on his chest laughing, then looking at him she confessed "Danny, Thanks for being so understanding and patient. I realized how much I loved you only after staying apart. I missed you every moment. I detest the idea of you marrying anyone else. I don't want to give you a reason to look at anybody anymore." She gave him a long passionate kiss. Danny could feel the change in her. Like a lioness defending her territory. He loved her for it all. He wanted her to love him back with all her might. They both longed to be together.

"Danny, what if I had not called you now?"

"I was waiting in the terrace contemplating how to pounce on you."

"You monster! I won't spare you" Susan joked.

"Yes! please don't spare me" laughed Danny pulling her closer.

"Let's go in" said Susan becoming aware of her surroundings.

"Let's have a long soak in the bathtub and refresh our memories."

"Someone may see us going in together" she said shyly.

They will only be happy, he reminded.

Danny's room had been tastefully done. On the wall hung the painting , they had liked at the art gallery depicting the spirit of India.

His room had a drawing room and a bedroom with a terrace. The drawing room was now serving him as his workstation. She could see his laptop and some files around it. In the corner stood the carved frame she had gifted him. On looking closer she found it had their photo accepting the consolation prize at the couple games and her pictures in a saree. Susan was touched by all this she had been so naïve not to have realized his sincere feelings.

He came closer and put his arms around her waist.

"You have made me wait for, too long sweetheart." He turned her around to face him "I love you and want you to be mine forever. Will you marry me?"

"I love you too, but I need some time" she said mischievously as she slipped and ran into the terrace. Danny was right behind her. He picked her up effortlessly. Susan was laughing till tears rolled down her cheeks.

"Naughty girl, you have all the time till we finish

our bath, and I am not letting you out till you say YES."

"I won't keep you waiting that long. I love you too and wish to marry you" replied Susan as she pulled Danny closer in the bathtub.

The next day was like a grand celebration at the breakfast table. Everyone had something funny to share in the role play.

Sam was utterly upset, he sat with a pout, hands crossed, and frown." What's wrong Sam? "enquired his mom.

"I am angry with Dan. I wanted to marry Susan." The whole room burst into laughter. Susan pulled him closer and assured him that she will remain his best friend. Sam hugged her and seemed happy with that proposition too. Just then a new visitor was announced. Danny held Susan's hand and led her out.

"Jia!" screamed Susan elated and surprised.

"Couldn't miss this for anything" chirped Jia.

"Well Ruby! You had asked me what I cherish from India the most? It's my best friend Jia" replied Susan.

Danny interrupted and reintroduced her "more

than just a friend , she is our Cupid ! Cupid from the East."

"Remember the fortune teller. He had told us; you will get the man of your dreams and he will be the best" reminded Jia .

"And no one can better, the best" boasted Danny as he put his arms around Susan then drawing all three in a warm hug.

It all seemed like a fairy tale, but they knew it was true. They were destined to be together. To share a bond, a bond for life.